LET US PREY

VIVIENNE SAVAGE

PAYNE AND TAYLOR

LET US PREY

WILD OPERATIVES #2

By Vivienne Savage
All material contained herein is Copyright © Payne &
Taylor 2015. All rights reserved.

***

http://www.viviennesavage.com

1

IAN

*N*ormally, I was a morning person, but the drone of a church sermon had me bleary-eyed and half asleep with my head dipping down little by little as the hour wore on. My grandmother had sweet-talked me into escorting her to Sunday worship for nefarious reasons.

She claimed the visit was to socialize, but I knew the truth. She wanted to introduce me to the divorced daughters of her friends. Once the preacher had his say, I was doomed to a fate of awkward conversation with middle-aged singles who would pretend to hang on every word I said while feigning interest in something besides my looks and income.

I sat beside Gram with my phone on vibrate in my pocket, expecting an important call from the Secretary of Defense to come at any moment. Or at least hoping for one. The government didn't stop for Sunday prayer sessions, and neither did war. As a retired Air Force Colonel and acting leader of a special squad of operatives, I retained certain privileges.

I was also a shapeshifter, an ability I inherited from my late grandfather. My fondest memories were of him sharing old tales about how our kind came to be. At my age, I should have had a son of my own, or even a daughter with whom I could share the story of Brother Eagle's gift to the people of the Ojibwe Nation.

"Please open your hymn books," a man announced to us from the pulpit.

My groan earned me a sharp elbow in the ribs from Gram, prompting me to hush and focus my attention elsewhere. *Ring, phone, ring,* I pleaded internally.

Once the singing began, led by the small choir up front, I scanned the church pews. I saw George Banks making eyes at his mistress, his wife unaware the entire time. A few teens texted with their phones in their laps while their disapproving parents stared at them. Chuckling, I nearly gave in and did the same... then I saw her.

A young woman sat alone in the rear of the church, isolated from the rest of the worshippers. She wore a plain white blouse and a dull, dove-grey skirt in a modest length. Its style wouldn't have flattered most women's curves, but her assets were so generous Houdini couldn't have hidden them. The perfect amount of hip and thick thighs. I knew without a doubt she'd have a bottom to match.

"Who's she?" I asked in a low murmur while the rest of the congregation sang the words to some hymn I didn't know.

Gram swatted me. "Ian," she hissed under her breath.

"Well?" I insisted.

"Her name is Leigh," she whispered.

"You're telling me nothing, Gram."

"She's a young woman who made poor choices, from what I hear."

From a woman who loved her share of gossip, I was disappointed by the ambiguity.

I spent the rest of the services stealing glances at Leigh, lost in her melancholy beauty and serene features. Church couldn't end fast enough, and when it did, I was the first from my seat. Following morning worship, the congregation gathered in the reception hall where they all enjoyed a spread of baked goods and casserole dishes. Gram had me carry in a peach cobbler as our donation prior to the service.

"Ian, where are you going?" I heard my grandmother calling.

"I'll be right back, Gram."

Two middle-aged women approached Leigh. One of them was Pastor Stevens' wife, a woman known for causing trouble. I tuned in to eavesdrop and pick up what I could as I narrowed the distance.

"Leigh, where's your contribution to our lunch? Don't you plan to stick around for once?" Lettie asked.

The other woman, Myrtle, made a disgusted sound like she was coughing up something in her throat. "I don't even know why you make the effort with her. She's only gonna dive out again, as usual."

Leigh blushed from the scooped neck of her blouse to the top of her ears. With her porcelain complexion and fair hair, there was no hiding the embarrassment. Whatever she said in reply was too low for my keen ears to pick up, but it was apparent she was excusing herself.

Our eyes met from across the foyer, and I caught my breath as if I'd been sucker-punched. Her grey irises were as pale as the rest of her, clear as a pre-dawn sky. She broke eye contact first and looked away.

The sorrow in Leigh's features called to the eagle inside me, and before I knew it, I was sprinting to the door. When I descended the steps, I saw her scurrying down the sidewalk at a brisk power walk. Two teen boys, one blond and one dark-haired, were hooting and making catcalls at her, being general pricks.

"Don't see why you're leaving so quickly. You need all the Jesus you can get!" the blond called to her.

I frowned and brushed past them.

"Oh shit," the dark-haired boy muttered.

"Why didn't you say MacArthur was nearby?" the other asked.

"Didn't see him," the blond whispered.

"Hold on a second!" I called to Leigh.

Leigh slowed ahead of me and peeked back over her shoulder, uncertainty on her face. "Me?"

"You shouldn't let them run you off, ma'am."

"Leigh," she corrected. "Leigh Denton."

"Ian MacArthur."

Her eyes went as round as two buttons. "You're a lot younger than I thought you were."

"Thanks? Uh, you seem to know about me, but I don't know the first thing about you."

"You're like a legend around here, Mr. MacArthur. They named the new food pantry after you, and the town library's named after your father."

A grin slipped onto my face. "Ian," I corrected her this time. "And they named it after my grandfather."

Leigh studied me then gazed at our surroundings with distrust, her big gray eyes darting to each side. "Did I do something wrong? Is that why they sent you after me?"

"Not at all. Actually, I was going to ask why you weren't sticking around."

Leigh fidgeted and avoided meeting my eyes. "They don't really like me, but I like to go hear the singing." She resumed her walk again, clutching a tattered grey, synthetic leather purse against her side. It probably cost her five dollars at the general store.

"And the luncheon?" I prodded, keeping pace with her.

"It's rude to take when you don't contribute. I'm not a mooch," she snapped back, revealing more with her defensiveness.

"Can't cook?" I asked. Maybe I was a legend in these parts, but she didn't seem impressed or willing to slow for me.

"I cook fine, I guess."

When I attempted to strike up conversation again, she picked up speed to leave me behind. She was a tall girl with a long stride, easily 5'10 or taller and just a couple inches below my own height. While her skirt was modest, it didn't conceal the strength of her calves and legs.

Taking the hint, I suppressed the urge to give chase. My eagle fought against my willpower, suddenly a screaming and raging beast. In all of my years, it had never reacted with as much intensity over a woman. Many shifters spent our entire lives looking for the right person — our soulmate so to speak — and in Leigh, I'd found mine. She crossed the next street and disappeared into a dilapidated home barely larger than my garden tool shack. Most houses in the poorer side of Quickdraw were uninhabitable tinder boxes ready to collapse.

Leigh remained on my mind during the walk back to the church. Someone had hurt that girl, making her cold and unreceptive to even innocent friendship. I found Gram waiting for me on the steps with a frown on her face.

"Ian, where were you?"

"I walked home the young woman Lettie and Myrtle were harassing. Saw some boys bothering her outside, too."

"Don't be getting yourself mixed up in other folks' problems, sweetheart. I had a word with Marjorie, and she says Leigh is all kinds of trouble. The criminal sort."

"Marjorie is also known to bouts of wild exaggeration," I pointed out.

"True enough, true enough," she admitted. "But most all here say the same. I just want you to be careful. You get into enough trouble with that team of yours."

"Gram, I love you, but I can make my own decisions. Are you ready to go home, or do you plan to hang around with the ladies?"

With frail and bony fingers, she pulled her shawl around her shoulders and gazed toward the car. "I'd like to go home, I think. It's too cold to socialize outdoors."

The girl with the pale eyes remained on my mind during the drive to my grandmother's home and throughout the distraction Gram made to redirect me. The cooking and cleaning got done, but I performed every task with my mind in another place. My thoughts returned to Leigh's curvy body. I'd always loved when girls were on the plump side.

"You're still thinking about Leigh, aren't you, Ian?"

I blinked away from my half-assed job at rinsing the plates for the dishwasher. "Sorry, Gram."

"Well?" With the assistance of her cane, she moved closer and lowered to one of the chairs in the kitchen's breakfast nook. Due to advanced arthritis, she couldn't wash dishes in the sink or lift them from the machine's basket without a struggle. When I returned to town, I made it a habit to pop in to do the small things for her until we could find a replacement aid. She fired the last one for stealing from the house, or rather, I did after Gram tipped me off to missing belongings and I logged into the nannycam for a look.

"Ian, I'm waiting." Old age hadn't made her patient.

"I think she's the one," I confessed.

"Ah." No arguments. No denials. Gram knew better than to fight against shifter instincts or to question the recognition of fated mates. Seventy years ago, she'd been one, too. "Well then, what do you plan to do? She's young and she's got many problems, Ian. Perhaps too many even for you."

I shook my head. "Everybody has problems, Gram, including you. I'm going to get to know her and find a way to help, and I don't care what anybody here says or how they gossip about it."

Gram gave me a reassuring smile. "Good. That's the boy I raised."

Leigh would be mine, and I'd do anything to convince her I was worthy of becoming hers.

~

I didn't have to ask around much to dig up the truth on Leigh. Two years ago, drama went down with the young woman renting my house when her stalker ex-husband keyed her car. After the cops got involved, I befriended the guys on the small, six-person police force and enlisted their help to watch out for her.

"What's the deal with Leigh Denton?" I asked.

Sergeant Jacob Hunt sighed. "Did she steal from you?"

"No! Christ. Jumping to conclusions a little, aren't you? No, she didn't steal from me. I'm asking because I witnessed some odd behavior the other day during church service, and I want to know why it happened."

"Leigh Denton is a mess of trouble, man. I know she's pretty, but you don't want to get caught up in her issues. Why don't you tap a contact or two and look at her police record—"

I cut him off before he began the usual spiel. "You

are my contact and you *are* the police. I want to hear what you have to say instead of pulling up her entire criminal background check, all right?"

"Point made. All right. You didn't hear all of the gritty details from me, but she lost custody of her infant about three months ago."

"Why?" I asked.

"The baby was born with neonatal withdrawal syndrome related to opiate use. Codeine is Leigh's drug of choice. Her boyfriend has a twenty-five year stretch at Ferguson Unit for dealing a whole plethora of narcotics."

Hunt's news hit me like a bucket of cold water. Lapsing into silence, I let the news wash over me and took a few moments to digest it all. When I saw Leigh, I didn't see a woman out for her next fix — I saw *and felt* a wounded soul crying for help. "What else?"

"She's got a juvie record for shoplifting, too. Stole a couple televisions from Wal-Mart. Got busted with a flat screen."

"How the hell do you steal a television from Wal-Mart?"

"Back when the Quickdraw Wal-Mart was new a couple years back, they didn't run as tight a ship as they do now. She went into the store, bought a television, and took it out to her friends in the parking lot. Then she returned to the store, fetched the second television, and cruised through the other exit doors with her receipt. She would have probably gotten away with it if she didn't try to hit the store up again after the shift change. Someone had reported strange behavior to loss prevention, and they were watching for any more suspicious acts."

Even as I took in all of the damning evidence against Leigh's character, something told me there was more to the story. I stroked my chin and gazed out the police department window. "What about her family?"

"Only child of deceased parents. Her mother, Louise Denton, was killed in a car wreck when she was five. Gregory Denton died a couple years back of laryngeal cancer. She lives in his old place on the North side."

"Tell me about the boyfriend." I used my phone to take notes.

"He was this good-for-nothing punk named Dennis James. When we busted him, he had enough prescription narcotics to stock his own pharmacy, Ian."

"Dealing for someone big or working his own business?"

"Who knows? One minute he was telling us all this shit about how he'd be out in a day; a few hours later, he's got his mouth shut tighter than a Baptist preacher's asshole."

I chuckled at the imagery. "What did the investigation turn up?"

"Turns out him and his boys were robbing elderly

people while they were asleep or out of the home and selling them on the market. He even stole from his own parents, and they're good, respectable people."

I thought back to the girl I caught pinching my grandmother's lorazepam one pill at a time. "Was Ms. Denton involved in the theft or distribution?"

"No, nothing we found or could prove. She seemed genuinely shocked when she heard the charges against him," Jacob said.

His words cleared the rest of my reservations. "Okay. So she wasn't shooting meth, she wasn't dealing, and as far as you know, she hasn't stolen anything since she was a kid."

"Why are you asking about this anyway?"

I had to think fast, searching for any excuse that would suffice and save me from admitting we were soul mates and sounding like I was out of my mind. "Gram needs a new home health aide and I thought about hiring Leigh. That's all."

Jacob gave me an uncertain look. "I'd keep a daily count of Mrs. MacArthur's medication then."

"I plan to after the last one we told you about, but I'm also a firm believer in giving people a chance."

"Let's hope your generosity doesn't bite you in the ass this time."

"Yeah, yeah, yeah. How's your boy doing anyway?" I swapped the subject to Hunt's seventeen-year-old son and his plans to enlist.

"Good, good. Danny took those practice placement tests, and they said he'd be a good fit for some of those technical jobs they have in the armed forces. Of course, he wants to take the language test and try his hand at linguistics."

"I was certain he was going to go with the Air Force. They take linguists, too, you know."

"Heh. Well, you know how boys are. Once his buddies going into the Army all called it the Chairforce, there wasn't much hope of getting him to go. I thought he'd at least enroll in college first," Jacob said.

I scowled at him. "There's less sitting involved than they'd have him believe. Either way, he'll get some good experience out of it and money for college. Maybe he'll come back to Quickdraw one day and work alongside you."

Jacob and I hung around his desk for a while longer before a call pulled him from the station to settle a fender bender dispute at the gas station. I went home to my personal office where I sat behind the computer and phoned a friend.

"Argus? Hope I caught you at a good time."

"Always have time for you, Ian. What can I do for you today?" he asked in his easygoing voice.

"I need you to draft up some legal paperwork for me about a job."

2

LEIGH

*J*ust before Daddy died, he signed his old Ford F-150 over into my name. Letting go of it for a few grand was one of the hardest decisions I ever had to make, but the money helped to make ends meet until I found a job.

With less than seven hundred dollars of it left to my name and few worldly possessions, I threw myself into finding gainful employment before I lost everything. Time at the library consumed most of the week, allowing me to fill out online applications at every business within fifty miles.

Days without Sophia passed into weeks and became months. The ache in my heart was a hollow, barren field where my baby belonged. Two days a week wasn't enough time, but I needed firm footing beneath me before the court returned her to my care. I failed her and *myself* when I didn't seek professional help during pregnancy.

Back then, I thought they'd judge me and take my baby away if I asked for help. In the end, they did it anyway by citing child endangerment. After CPS took her away, I spent the first weeks cursing the medical staff who reported me and laying blame everywhere but the place it belonged. Myself.

The driver of the carpool to Ferguson Unit honked from the side of the road. I ran out and joined two other women in the backseat after passing ten dollars to the driver. An hour later, an intimidating prison loomed ahead of us, a massive brick facility with two layers of perimeter fencing and harsh razor wire. Impassive guards armed with AR-15s watched us from towers in passing.

I shivered and scurried along with the rest of the flock, feeling like a sheep herded to pasture. The other ladies wore makeup, but my face was bland and intentionally unappealing. They wore dresses and tight-fitting tops. I wore jeans and a light cardigan over a V-neck, which I fastened before entering the facility.

The humiliating shakedown procedures were just part of the sacrifice I made to see Dennis. I turned my pockets inside out, set my shoes in the bin for the x-ray machine, and walked through the metal detector with my hands raised. A female officer ran her fingers down my body, sliding her palms down my spine then the backs of her hands down my ass. Her smaller build placed her at an inconvenience and forced her to stand on tiptoe and lean uncomfortably close to reach around my thicker frame. Once she was satisfied I didn't have drugs and cigarettes stuffed into my meager bra, she shooed me to get out of her line.

I was shuffled into a visitation room for an impersonal meeting behind glass walls. I sat nervously on my chair with my hands folded over my lap. I'd never gone into a prison before in all of my life, but the dismal, gray-painted cinder blocks and dirty floor depressed me.

I tensed the moment Dennis entered the room and sat opposite me with a thick pane of glass between us.

He looked as good as I remembered, with full lips, chiseled features, and a strong jaw. I'd always loved his cocoa brown skin and the contrast between our complexions. At a glance, I could tell he'd picked up some weight and broadened his shoulders with muscle. Figures in the penitentiary he'd have nothing better to do than work out, but the plain white uniform didn't do his athletic body the justice it deserved.

"What took you so long to finally come here and visit me? You don't write and you didn't register to accept calls from me."

"I don't have a vehicle anymore, Dennis. I had to sell Daddy's truck a couple months ago to make ends meet."

The honest truth didn't seem to satisfy him. "Yeah, all right. That don't explain why you didn't register. I could have been calling you by now, baby."

The last affection I had for Dennis died on the day he'd gotten himself locked away for a quarter of a century on an unnecessary crime. I hated knowing Sophia would grow up without a father for the mistakes he made. We should have been raising her together.

"I've been too busy trying to find a job to sit at home on the phone, Dennis. Besides, I don't know how to register," I lied.

"Damn. Fair enough." His brown eyes drifted to the inmate beside him. The guy's family had purchased him a pile of chips and four icy Cokes from the over-priced vending machine.

"I came to talk to you about Sophia," I spoke up to direct the conversation.

"Buy me a Coke first, Leigh."

I shook my head. "Don't have it on me."

"What? You can't even buy me a soda while you're here?"

"I don't have the money," I repeated, voice low. "No one told me I could bring quarters for the machines."

"It's a fucking buck, Leigh. You mean to tell me you don't have a goddamn dollar to spare for me?"

"I wouldn't even be here if I didn't carpool with a group. I gave them ten dollars to get here." I had an electric bill to pay and groceries to buy. While he received three hot meals and a cot courtesy of Texas, I was left to fend for myself.

"Then what the hell are you doing here, girl? It's not like you even tried to pretty yourself up," he fussed at me. I swear he said those things just to be an asshole and hurt me.

"Pretty myself up for a prison visit? Like I said, I came to talk about Sophia and getting her back. Or at least seeing her more often." Had he even been listening to me? "Can't you talk to them? They're your parents, Dennis."

"You know how Ma and Dad are. I can't tell them nothin' from in here."

"Tell them to let me see her more."

"Hell, Leigh, you see her more than I do. You think they bring her up here for me to see her?"

"Yeah, well whose damn fault is that?" I snapped back.

A couple of prison guards in stiff gray suits glanced our way. When the male officer moved as if he intended to come over, I dropped my voice again.

"Listen, Dennis. Sophia is my baby. Ours. She doesn't belong with her grandparents. She needs a mom, and them keeping her from me when I've been clean isn't for her benefit. They're doing it because they're pissed at us."

"Bitch, are you even clean for real this time? How

many days did you tell me you were done and not to get you any more pills, but the moment I offered a bottle, you were ready to take them?" he mocked me.

"I *am* clean," I hissed. Counting backward from ten in my head helped me calm down. "I haven't touched so much as an aspirin since they discharged me from the hospital." I must have looked hostile, because the officer was on his way back again. I stood up from my seat and beat him to the punch. "Our visit is over. I'm leaving. Don't expect to see me back again."

I spent the rest of the two hours outside on the curb, the occasional passing car the only witness to my silent tears. Eventually, the shudders ended and I was able to embrace a future without Dennis in my life. In our lives, if I could pull it together and meet the requirements set by the court.

I had to have a job, and I needed it yesterday.

~

"Thanks again for the ride," I said to Kelly. The blonde woman in the driver's seat smiled at me.

"No problem, sweetheart. You email me next time you need a ride up there."

Positive I'd never go back, I smiled and nodded. "Sure." I waved and let myself inside, kicked off my shoes, and locked the door behind me.

My dad's home had seen better days, and with him gone, I couldn't replace the leaking roof. But it was a house, and it was better than some people had. Once I secured a job, I'd be able to change things and do him proud. I'd get the windows replaced and a new roof over my head. I'd have a new bedroom door to replace the one the cops knocked down when they arrested Dennis. I'd need the floors covered in something eventually, so Sophia wouldn't have to crawl on hard cement.

A quick shower let me wash the stink of the prison from my skin and hair. I could still smell it, the stench of a few thousand men and sweaty guards in a cement box without any air circulation. I shivered, remembering the way some of the inmates had stared at me with lust in their eyes despite my perceived plain appearance.

Someone beat on the door just as I toweled off in the tiny closet of a bathroom. I squeezed into panties, shorts, and an off- the- shoulder t-shirt then stepped barefoot into the narrow hall. I twisted my hair into a bun on the way to answer it. My tee revealed my lack of a bra, but without much on top to warrant wearing one all of the time, I thought I was safe from any lookie-loos wanting to steal a peek. My pear-shaped body meant I carried all of my junk in the trunk.

Caution made me pause before opening the door, and a quick glance through the parted window shades revealed an unfamiliar black SUV parked alongside the road. I frowned and angled my body for a peek at the stoop.

Ian MacArthur stood on the porch, his hands folded behind his back. The sexy military vet wore a black leather jacket and dark shades over his unusual, strangely colored eyes. The t-shirt on his body stretched taut over every muscular ridge, a second skin in navy blue.

"What the hell is he doing here?" I whispered. The next sharp rap on the door made me jerk back; then a surge of courage prompted me to crack it open and peek out at him. "Hello?"

"Good evening, Leigh. This a good time for a talk?"

"I just got out the shower."

"I can wait for you to get dressed," he said pleasantly.

"I am dressed." I paused and looked down at my chunky thighs. My current state of dress was inappropriate for meeting with the grandson of our town's founder. "What do you want, Mr. MacArthur?"

"To offer you a job."

I opened the door to stare at him. "Bullshit."

"Give me a second and hear me out. I'm told you're in need of a job. As luck would have it, I need an employee."

It was too good to be true, the perfect solution to my problem at the ideal time. I gazed at the handsome man on my doorstep and felt a cold stab of shame streak through me when I realized he could see the room behind me. The rough concrete floors needed another sweep, but it was the least of my troubles when I had a spreading water stain on the ceiling.

"May I come in to talk?"

"We can talk out here." I scurried outside and shut the door behind me.

"I want to offer you a job. You see, I work out of town and my grandmother's getting up in her years. The home health agency only gives her so many hours on the weekends, and she won't hire a housekeeper through the week or allow me to do it for her."

A flash of rage shot through me. "Housekeeping? Is this a joke? Is that it? Did you come to have a laugh at me too because no one wants to hire me for a real job in this shithole?"

"Leigh—"

"Fuck you, Mr. MacArthur. You can go to hell along with everyone else."

I slammed the door in his face before the tears began, and within moments, I was reduced to uncontrollable sobs. Damn him. Damn him and everyone else laughing behind my back. In the privacy of my own home, I wiped at the hot flood trickling down my cheeks and succumbed to my anguish. I needed a legitimate, tax-paying job, and under the table work cleaning bathtubs wouldn't cut it.

Maybe I brought it on myself, but why couldn't they just allow me to wallow in my own well-deserved punishment without rubbing in the salt?

"Leigh?" Ian's soft voice penetrated my flimsy door. A glance through the peephole showed the man hadn't moved. "I only want to talk to you for a moment. I'm not here to make fun or judge you. If you'd just let me come in for a moment to talk..."

"Is it a real job?"

"A real job," he confirmed.

I opened the door for him again after I wiped my face. "Okay."

When Ian entered and removed his glasses, he barely gave my sparsely decorated home a glance. His eyes lingered on me, resting on my face instead of my thick thighs and single bare shoulder. His features held no judgment and lacked the mockery I expected.

"Thank you. I brought the paperwork with me, and you can keep it to review overnight if you'd like, or sign it now and I'll take it with me. Choice is yours."

He offered me a manila folder filled with official looking papers and not like something he'd typed up at home. The fancy letterhead and watermark featured a wolf's head logo from the law offices of Argus Prescott.

"I'm sorry for losing my temper and slamming the door," I apologized. "Can I get you anything? I have..." *Nothing. I have nothing to offer him except tap water.* Soda wasn't in my budget lately. Food stamps could only get a single person so far.

"Water's great."

I set the papers on the coffee table — a handmade, beautiful piece my dad had carved and assembled himself about ten years ago — then gestured for him to have a seat on the paisley green sofa. I returned with his glass of ice water and joined him.

"Thank you, Leigh. Why don't you take a moment to review those while I'm here in case you have any questions."

My hands shook as I lifted the thin folder and flipped it open for a look. Responsibilities of the job and daily duties, a schedule, protocols for calling in sick, and a close set of rules to follow. He'd outlined everything professionally, complete with information about healthcare and vacation days.

"Vacation days?" I asked.

"Twenty-one days a year with two weeks advance notice so I can be there for her in your stead. I expect you to be at Gram's place five days a week. You've got two paid sick days a month, but they'll add up and won't expire so make them count. But keep in mind, I'd prefer if my grandmother wasn't made ill because you forced yourself on the job with the flu, got it?"

"Okay. What's my pay?"

"Fifteen dollars an hour to start, paid every Friday.

If you like it a month from now, I'll raise you to twenty."

Tears stung my eyes. "I... you want to pay me twenty dollars an hour to clean your grandmother's house?" Sniffling and wiping my cheeks, I tried to maintain a calm expression. I couldn't. Emotion burned my throat and tears spilled over my face too quickly to be dried for long. "This isn't a joke?" I repeated again.

"It isn't a joke."

"Why help me? Why?"

"Well, I hope you're not too mad at me, but I asked about you, and the way I see it, there's a little girl depending on her mama finding a stable job. And I have a legally blind grandmother with rheumatoid arthritis. We need each other, right?" Ian asked.

I wanted to throw my arms around him and smother his neatly groomed face in kisses. "Thank you. Thank you so much, Mr. MacArthur—"

"Ian," he said again with a pleasant smile on his handsome face. "Just call me Ian."

"Ian," I agreed. Shock made it impossible to convey my gratitude without floundering for words. I repeated the simplest ones. "Thank you."

"If you don't mind, I'd like to ask you a couple of questions for my own curiosity."

My belly sank a little, like a lead weight hit the bottom of my gut. "Okay."

"I know you've had some drug problems, Leigh. I want to believe it won't be a problem again. I'm not one to mince words, so I'm sorry if I offend you but... what happened? Did your boyfriend get you hooked?"

"It *won't* be a problem again," I quickly blurted out, too defensive. "This is a bit of a long story, and it's no excuse, but it started in college. I played volleyball until I blew out my knee at the start of my junior year. Surgery was out of the question because my dad was fighting cancer."

"Right. You probably couldn't afford two sets of medical bills," Ian deduced.

"Yes. So my doc prescribed me some codeine while I did physical therapy. I got into therapeutic horseback riding at this ranch at the edge of town, volunteering to help the kids in exchange for riding lessons and time with the therapist. Loved it. At the start of my senior year, Dad's cancer got worse. I dropped out to care for him and the ranch closed down due to lack of funds. They weren't getting enough money to care for the horses even though the therapist and trainer volunteered their time. Because I'd dropped out of school, I lost my student insurance plan."

Ian shook his head. "I wish I'd known about the ranch's troubles. I knew they shut down, but never heard about why. I must have been away at the time."

"Yeah. It was really sad. I couldn't afford my doctor or a new therapist, so Dennis supplied me with codeine. I was too stupid to ask where it came from. Or I didn't care. I was hurting and always needed one more to get through a day with Dad. The laryngectomy didn't help him, you know? The surgeon missed some of the cancer, and it metastasized to his lymph nodes. He came home here to die instead of hospice in a facility."

I swallowed and focused on my lap, fearing if I looked up at Ian, I'd see the judgment in his handsome face. Stealing a quick glance revealed compassion instead.

"I wanted to get help, Ian. I did. By the time I realized I had a problem, I was pregnant. I tried to kick it a dozen times on my own, but I was so afraid they'd take her from me. If I had it to do over again, I'd have never started taking them." Time had given my knee the chance to heal, but I'd probably benefit from resuming therapy.

Ian's fingers brushed the top of my hand in a reassuring stroke and left goose bumps in their wake. "It's behind you now, Leigh. What about your boyfriend?"

"We're done. I don't even know what I saw in him anymore. His parents used to love me, you know?" These days, I couldn't get them to talk to me unless it was my scheduled visit to see Sophia.

"What about the theft? Do I have to worry about you stealing?"

I shook my head. "I stole a television a couple years

back when my dad lost his job and we fell on hard times. Welfare office was going to take forever to process our case, and your food pantry didn't exist back then."

"So you stole a TV to sell for money to buy food?"

My cheeks flared with heat. "It only made things worse for us and was a dumb thing to do. I can't take it back and undo it, but I'll always regret the way he looked at me when we had to go to court. I shamed him and myself trying to take the easy way out."

Ian and I talked a while longer while I reviewed the rest of the papers. At the conclusion of our meeting, he wished me a good evening and made his way outside onto the pebbled road. He was gone and out of sight a few minutes later, leaving me to marvel over my change in luck.

I finally had the chance I needed to earn Sophia back. My prayers had been answered.

*M*y change in luck was too good to be true, leading me to believe I'd make the two-mile walk to Mrs. MacArthur's house to meet an old lady who loathed me on sight. I was wrong. She drew me into a motherly embrace and kissed my cheek before inviting me inside.

Two hours later, I finished cleaning the kitchen from top to bottom. I reached all the nooks and crannies Ian neglected whenever he visited to help. Afterward, I tried to move on to the master bedroom of the small six room ranch style home, but Mrs. MacArthur dragged me into the living room and made me sit with her.

We watched soap operas until noon then I made her lunch, which she insisted on sharing.

"Sweetheart, if you're going to make lunch for me,

you have to make something for yourself. It's just not right to watch someone else eat."

"Mrs. MacArthur, I don't think your grandson wants me eating your food while I'm here."

"Baby, my grandson didn't hire you to be my maid. He wants you to give me company, and *I* say I don't like to eat alone."

I made another sandwich for myself and took out fish to thaw for dinner. By the time Ian arrived from a day of work in Houston, doing whatever it was rich and sexy guys like him did, I'd whipped together a delicious meal for the three of us to enjoy.

After we ate, I scrubbed the dishes and cleaned my mess. I kissed Mrs. MacArthur, who firmly insisted on me calling her Betty, on the cheek and hugged her tight.

"Will I see you at the same time tomorrow?" she asked.

"Of course."

I left her house with a big smile on my face and a feeling of self-worth I never knew was possible. Before my feet touched the sidewalk, the door opened again to frame Ian's tall body.

"If you wait just a sec, I can give you a ride home, Leigh."

His black Escalade chirped when he released the door locks by remote. A second later, the lights flashed and the engine powered on with a roar. I stared at him.

"Mr. Mac— Ian, you don't have to drive me home. I like the walk."

"I'd like to talk to you," he countered.

I was positive he intended to fire me for some unknown transgression. My mind jumped to every worst possible conclusion until he stepped from his grandmother's house precisely a minute later and flashed me a great big grin.

It wasn't fair for one man to be so damned good looking. Ian's high cheekbones made him resemble his late grandfather the most. There were old black and white photos of our town founder in the house. He was a handsome Native American man with flowing black hair past his shoulders and equally pale eyes. It must have been a family trait.

"So, tell me how you like it." Ian fastened his seatbelt and waited for me to do the same. I clicked in quickly.

"Betty and I had an awesome time. I think she sees better than she lets you believe though. You wouldn't believe how she moves around the kitchen."

"Nah, she's just good at fooling you. You'll catch on," he assured me.

Tucked into his car, I was keenly aware of everything about him. His cologne was subtle, a scent I associated with cool wind snaking between sweet autumn trees. Resisting the temptation to lean over and breathe him in became an exercise in willpower.

"You said you wanted to talk," I prompted.

"When's your next appearance in court?"

"I'm supposed to report having a job by next week, then we reconvene next month. The judge only gave me so much time to prove I can make a stable environment for Sophia." I nervously bit my lower lip and stole another glance at my new boss. "I guess I have the job part done."

"Then I'd better give you an advance on your paycheck so you can get a head start on providing the stable environment part."

"An advance?"

He pulled out his wallet and a giant roll of cash bigger than anything I ever saw outside of a bank. I stared at him in amazement as he handed over ten crisp hundred dollar bills.

"What about the taxes?" I asked lamely. Math wasn't my preferred subject of study in school, but I was positive 40 hours at 15 dollars wouldn't add up to a grand.

Ian chuckled. "Well, we'll just pretend between you and me that I paid you in exact change. Don't count on it next time though. I'll pay by check and you can open a bank account to cash it."

"Okay," I agreed while focusing on my lap. It was a better alternative to staring at my boss and melting over the way his grin crinkled his pale eyes at the corners. Or how he had just the perfect amount of scruff on his tanned face.

"I have big expectations out of you, Leigh. I trust you won't relapse, but if you ever need to talk, I want you to call me, all right?" He passed me a business card with a U.S. Air Force eagle emblem above a blue banner announcing him as a veteran.

COLONEL IAN MACARTHUR, RETIRED

MACARTHUR SECURITY, CO.

(936) 555-5555

"There's my cell phone number. You're welcome to contact me at any time and any hour. I'll always answer if I can."

"Why are you being so good to me?"

Ian pulled out from the drive without answering right away. The houses passed by outside and the sky dimmed.

"My ancestors believed in strengthening the community and the people who lived in it. I look at you and I see a woman striving to make positive changes in her life. That's something I respect, Leigh."

The differences between the north and south sides of Quickdraw were vast; our main toad bisected the town into two distinct areas. Betty MacArthur lived on the south side and only a brisk walk from the town police department, which shared a building with the fire department and city hall. On my side, there weren't as many pretty gardens and the homes were smaller.

"Do you want a ride in the morning?" The street-lamp outside my house flickered as he pulled up. Further down the road, a group of teens collected near another street corner with their hands in their pockets. They watched us like hawks.

"No, I like the walk. Really," I assured him. "It wakes me up and helps get me going."

"All right. It'll make me feel better if you wait for me in the evening though. The news is probably spreading through town right this moment, but there was a shooting only a couple blocks over sometime last night. Heard about it on my way out to work this morning."

"A shooting in my neighborhood?" The chilling news didn't surprise me.

"Yep. Looked like a drug deal gone bad or something. No one died, but the cops took both of them into custody."

"Thanks, Ian. Anyway, Betty is amazing, and I'm glad you trust me with her care. I loved hearing her stories."

"Good. I'll see you tomorrow on my way in from work. Take care." He paused, the moment stretching for eternity between us. "I'm proud of you, Leigh. You're doing great."

"Thanks," I whispered. "Bye, Ian." Stunned, I

stepped from the car and barely shut the door with shaky fingers. Proud of me? He barely knew me.

He lingered until I was safely inside and the door was shut. After locking up, I ran my fingers over the green bills in my hand and wept myself to exhaustion. My life was finally turning around, and I had my own personal guardian angel to thank for it.

~

IAN

*L*eigh haunted my memories long after I returned home, a persistent force invading my thoughts until I stripped out of my clothes and walked onto the rear patio. I hit the pause button on the security camera first — I didn't need a digital record of what I planned to do.

I let the eagle overtake me, inflicting a sharp crack of pain to both of my arms, snapping my bones and reshaping me into a compact, feathered body. Whenever I left the ground behind and took to the air, the world around me gained a new level of clarity.

Flying past Russ and Dani's house gave me a glimpse of her with their new horse, Daisy. Russ was building a barn while his girlfriend of two years hosed the mare down after a ride. I envied him when we realized Dani was his fated mate, their binding obscured by the lingering traces of his grief for the one he'd already lost.

Dani peered up and shielded her eyes against the setting sun. She waved to me and I called back to her in return. I left them behind and soared toward the town.

Quickdraw wasn't the same place of my childhood. Sickness had infested its soul. The wind carried me over to the south side where Gram lived. I wish she'd stay with me, but she wanted to have neighbors in walking distance. She wanted to see children playing ball in their yards and walking dogs down the street.

I wanted Leigh's baby to become the great-grand-child Gram deserved. As my flight path brought me toward the north side, I scanned the ground below me and took in the sight. Wealth and comfort bled away to barren, sandy yards and unpaved streets. Circling around gave me the chance to scout the area near Leigh's home and descend to a light post at the street corner.

Criminal activity bustled at her neighbor's home. A car pulled up and stalled in front of it, waiting until a little boy ran down with a baggie of weed. The kid, no more than seven or eight, took the money back up to his father.

A scrawny, malnourished dog trotted down the road with swinging teats close to dragging the dusty road. Leigh's door opened to frame her in shorts and an oversized tee. She held a small bowl in her hand piled with rice. When she approached the road, the dog paused and met her halfway. The animal snapped up the offering.

"I wish I had more for you," she said.

"Hey, Leigh! Why do you bother feedin' that ugly thing? Why don't you let me shoot it and put it out of its misery?" one of the men called from her neighbor's porch.

Leigh shook her head. "Actually, I'm thinking of keeping her. She comes this way every couple of days, and I don't think anyone owns her."

"Bitch, you don't even got a job. How you gonna take care of a dog?"

"I do now," she called back. She ran her fingers over the dog's floppy ears and straightened from her crouch. Her eyes raised to me then became large as saucers. "Holy shit, it's a bald eagle!"

"I'll be damned. It is," one of the neighbors said.

I came down closer to her and glided to the low chain-link fence around her house. Leigh gasped and didn't move while I preened my flight feathers. A handful of yards distanced us, but my eagle craved contact. I wanted to feel her fingers over my wings and to touch my beak against her soft cheek.

"I wish I had a camera... it's beautiful," Leigh murmured.

"Better get your mutt inside before the bird takes a bite out of it," one of the guys called.

"Eagles don't eat dogs," Leigh argued.

"Bet if the fucker was a rat dog, it would've taken off with it by now." The guys howled with laughter while Leigh backed away with the canine.

The reservation in her eyes told me she didn't want to go inside. She wanted to watch me as much as I wanted to watch her.

"I'm telling you. There ain't no reason a big bird like that's sitting around except to find its next meal, Leigh."

Gray eyes watched me the entire time she led the hungry dog up her porch steps. After the mongrel was safely indoors, Leigh returned with a disposable camera.

"I can't believe he's still here. Two shots left..."

The neighbors moved on to another conversation. A woman brought them fresh beer and another drug-seeking customer arrived. Leigh glanced at them with morose eyes and sighed.

Desperate to take her sadness away, I glided to the dusty walking stone in front of her porch. She shrieked and stumbled back against the door, banging her hip in the process.

"Leigh, you okay?" the concerned neighbor woman called.

"Shit. I thought the thing was attacking her," one of the guys commented.

"Maybe I should shoot it," one of the guys threatened.

"No!" Leigh screamed at them. "It's not doing anything."

A couple men chuckled. "You ain't no Disney princess, lil mama. Let us chase it off before it hurts you."

"Fuck you," she seethed at him, revealing a stubborn streak. The young woman approached despite their warnings. With my beak closed and tilted down, I watched her hesitate until I closed the gap and touched my feathered head against her bare knee.

"Oh, my God. Oh, my God," she whispered under her breath.

"Maybe it's sick," one of them speculated. When I didn't fly into a vicious rage or attack, they lost interest in watching. Our moment became truly ours, and then her fingers were against the nape of my feathered neck.

"You're so big," she breathed out loud. My mind traveled to other places, wondering if she'd say the same thing in bed once I was above her and our naked limbs were twined. The dangerous line of thought tempted my beast, so I pulled away before I lost all control. Leigh startled back as I snapped out my wings. A powerful flap lifted me into the air, where I circled twice before riding an air current away from her home.

My survey of north Quickdraw yielded similar results of criminal behavior and sketchy individuals. Why weren't the police doing anything?

I returned to my house before absolute darkness fell and showered once I was inside. The memory of her touch didn't fade.

Leigh. She was mine, and soon, I'd be hers too.

4

LEIGH

One Month Later

*B*etty and I passed out candy alone for Halloween until Ian arrived in a Captain America costume. Petunia lay on the porch beside us, large and near the end of her pregnancy. We'd have puppies soon.

I eyeballed Ian from top to bottom as he kissed his grandmother's cheek. The fitted costume suited his physique, sexy as all get out and too authentic to be cheap.

"I think I'll be going inside now," Betty said. "This cold is too much for my arthritis, you know."

"It's barely a breeze," I protested.

She ignored me and continued inside. "I'll see you Tuesday, Leigh. Good luck. Goodnight, Ian."

Without thinking anything else of it, I turned back to Ian. His costume deserved my attention. "I wish I knew you were going to dress up. I would have done the same," I teased, nudging his ribs with my elbow. "Why *are* you dressed up?"

"I visit Texas Children's Hospital each year on Halloween," he explained. "It's sort of a tradition between me and some of the other guys in my squad. We go on down to Houston and tell stories to the kids."

"How long have you been doing this sort of thing?"

"This is the fourth year for me," he admitted. Petunia lumbered over and set her face on his knee until he scratched behind her ears. My dog loved him.

"Isn't Cap another branch and rank?" I asked innocently. I unwrapped a Hershey's kiss and held it in my mouth until it melted.

"Well, yeah, technically..."

Ian had a fresh shave for his Halloween role, and if he wore his hair long, he would have been a dead ringer for his grandfather. My gentle ribbing brought out a blush, its warm hue complementary to the exotic complexion he'd inherited from his grandmother and grandfather. I had discovered Betty was biracial, too; the daughter of a white man and black woman, but so fair-skinned it wasn't easily apparent. I eagerly listened to her stories of love existing during a time when society was against them.

"The part in the movie was definitely miscast," I

said. After unwrapping a second chocolate and offering it to him from my fingers, I held my breath when he took it without hesitation, his lips closing around my fingertips. Ian and I had a kind of easy-going flirtation between us.

"You think so, huh?"

"I know so."

We hung out together for an hour longer as roving bands of children came for treats. My biggest regret was that I couldn't take Sophia to the yearly Trick or Treat social at the church in an adorable costume.

Ian jingled the keys to his SUV. "Guess you're off the clock now officially. Thanks for hanging around past your usual hours."

"Are you kidding? We had a blast. I love decorating for the holidays. Any holiday, really." We piled into the car and buckled our seatbelts. When we reached my neighborhood, we passed the usual gang of teenagers standing beneath a dimmed street lamp. We both knew what they were doing, but the local police didn't care about the small fry dealers.

"How do you feel about Monday?" Ian asked to break the silence.

"I always have trouble sleeping the night before a visit with her. Every other weekend isn't enough. I want to see her every day and let her know I haven't forgotten her and haven't abandoned her."

"It's because you love her, Leigh."

"Sometimes I worry I need her more than she needs me." Until her big gray eyes gazed up at me with something resembling recognition during my last visit. "I miss her so bad, Ian. I just wish they'd let me bring her home for a few hours. Even a night. Why do they think I'd go through all of these hoops just to hurt her? I mean, on Monday the judge is just going to review my case and see I fulfilled all his requirements, right?"

"It takes time to regain trust, sweetheart. But you're doing the right thing now playing it by their rules. Look at how far it's gotten you." He parked in front of my house.

I nodded, feeling foolish for the tears stinging my eyes. Only a few more days, and my nightmare would be over. Sniffling, I wiped my face with the back of my hand, then was taken by surprise when Ian pulled me into his arms. I became hyperaware of too many things at once: the earthy, familiar scent of juniper and woodsy pine I associated with him, his strength, how perfect we fit together when I set my cheek against his shoulder, and how much I wished he saw me as more than a charity case to save.

"Do you have a ride over?" he asked.

Once my emotions were under complete control, I leaned back from Ian and separated. "It's a ten minute walk. Their house is just up on Amarillo Drive." Uphill into a nicer area of town.

"What about to the courthouse?"

"Uh..." Shit. I drove Daddy's truck last time, and without it, I didn't have a way to reach the courthouse twenty miles away.

"As luck would have it, my schedule is clear Monday."

Ian probably had some sexy girlfriend waiting for him at home. Most of the town, including me, didn't know much about his personal life. And any attempts to wheedle information out of Betty resulted in absolute failure. He struck me as a private individual with a big heart, and ever since our evening ritual began, he'd never once hit on me in the car. Never made a pass at me.

Of course not, I thought, suddenly irritated with myself. Ian was a real gentleman, the kind of guy idealized in time period romances depicting the south. Once I reminded myself his interest in me was purely charitable, I suppressed the urge to do anything more than lean across the truck's center console for a hug. I threw both arms around Ian, catching him off guard with the ferocity of my embrace.

"Thank you, Ian. *Thank you.*"

"It was my pleasure, Leigh. I..." He squeezed me a little tighter, imparting a sense of safety I'd missed. Why was the second hug better than the first? "Maybe it's wrong to ask now, but I wondered if you'd like to join me for dinner Monday somewhere. Alone and without Gram."

My heart stuttered and missed a beat. "Dinner?"

"Yeah, an evening out."

I swallowed nervously, fearing I misread a friendly celebration offer. "Like a date?" I whispered.

"Like a date. We could catch a movie after your hearing, unless they let you take Sophia home with you right off. We'll just swing dinner somewhere kid-friendly then."

As if to compensate for seeming to stop, my heart slammed wildly in my chest, pulsing so hard I could barely hear him above the rushing sound filling my ears. "A date?"

"I do believe that's what the cool kids call it these days."

"Yes. Yes. I want to." I really wanted to, so much I was afraid I'd ruin the moment by speaking something foolish out loud. To spare myself any embarrassment, I turned my face toward his cheek and brushed my lips against his skin. "My hearing is at nine forty-five." I leaned back to look at him.

"I'll be here by eight o'clock."

I stepped out of the SUV then gently lifted Petunia from the rear seat. Ian waited for us to get inside the house and close the door before he drove away.

Between his advance bonus and my first couple paychecks, Daddy's old house looked like a home again. Ian had helped me paint and seal the ugly cement floors a week ago. The marbleized appearance gleamed with a smooth finish beneath a few tidy floor rugs. I couldn't show him enough gratitude for taking me to the store.

My roof no longer leaked. He and his friend Russ spent one sunny autumn afternoon on the ladders and did the repairs without charging me until I forced them to accept the cost of supplies.

"I can't wait to bring Sophia home." I had outlet covers, a secondhand crib, and everything needed to welcome her. Betty was eager to meet my child and swore up and down Sophia was welcome to attend my work duties with me every day. As Ian didn't have children, she looked forward to having a baby in her company.

My life was really taking a turn for the better, and I owed it all to one stubborn man named Ian MacArthur. Grinning, I kicked off my shoes and locked the door behind me. I was on cloud nine.

As part of my recovery, I'd become a creature of habit and took comfort in following the same routine each night. Following my shower, I fetched a yogurt cup from the fridge and settled cross-legged on the couch to watch the local news. As I toweled my hair dry, the weather forecast was interrupted by a Breaking News report.

"Ferguson Unit is under a prison lockdown following a riot that took place this evening. Correctional officers were forced to deploy chemical agents to regain control of the recreation facilities and report no officers were harmed during the events. Numerous injuries and three fatalities are reported at this time among the inmate population. TDCJ has not released any names, pending notification of the families."

My brow creased as the news carried on without any further elaboration.

Although I had no true reason to worry about him, I laid down in bed hoping Dennis hadn't been one of those inmates on the recreation yard. By morning, I was in better spirits and able to enjoy the brisk stroll to the James residence. The couple who could have once been my in-laws lived in a quaint, cottage-style home on the south side of the main road.

They'd given Dennis everything, so I couldn't imagine what led him to dealing drugs. His father answered the door as usual, looking worn and unkempt. I'd seen him this way before after a night of beers with his friends.

"Good morning, Mr. Ja—"

He cut me off before I finished my greeting. "We're not up for supervising your visit today, Leigh. Go home."

"What do you mean I can't see her? It's my day. I get four hours today," I argued.

"Not today, Leigh."

"Why not?" I demanded hotly. His hangover had nothing to do with my child and me.

"Dennis is dead, and we'd like to mourn him in peace, without you here to remind us why he was in prison in the first place."

The fire and anger dimmed in an instant. "What? But no one called. No one told me."

"Our son was killed in a riot last night, or don't you care?"

"I..." He'd torn the rug out from under me. My eyes filled with unshed tears and I stared at him, wordlessly opening and closing my mouth. Dennis was dead. Killed and gone in the blink of an eye. My child was without a father.

"Go on now, Leigh. You're not welcome here."

Sour acid burned up my throat, but I swallowed back the urge to throw up. I didn't recall much of the walk home. Sharp pain radiated through my chest and consumed my very soul. All I could think about was Sophia, and what this meant for her. Dennis had been condemned to twenty-five years, but he would have managed a mediocre presence. Now she had no father. Not even a deadbeat to flit through her childhood like a passing shadow in the night.

IAN

"*H*ey, do you remember when this asshole promised we'd all go on an escort to Iran without even asking if we were interested?" Russ asked.

"Who doesn't?" Sasha replied.

"You got paid for it," I grumbled. "I couldn't help it was an all or nothin' deal."

"He's still at it. Guess who got roped into an afternoon of roof repairs a couple weeks back?" Russ pointed a thumb at himself. "Ian's turned into a true angel of benevolence since retiring. I expect he'll open his own soup kitchen for the homeless by Christmas."

Russ quieted down once he found himself on the receiving end of a dirty look.

Since my retirement, the group of us met at least once a month to unwind and play catch-up on each other's lives. My house was preferred for the pool I'd had built last year, unless we hung out at Sasha's penthouse in Houston. The youngest member of our team, a marine named Nadir, remained in active duty and was missing from our get-together.

Taylor's feline instincts let him hone in on my discomfort. Like a true jackass, he picked up where Russ left off. "So, what's happening with the hot girl?"

Playing dumb, I shrugged and raised my beer to my lips for another swig. "What hot girl?" They'd never let me live it down if they knew my eagle had responded to a girl less than half my age.

"The blonde with the booty," Taylor replied, gesturing with his hands for emphasis. "The one taking care of your grandmother."

"Ooh, spill it, Ian." Sasha flicked a bottle cap into the trash. Her lazy sprawl on the lawn chair was reminiscent of her lioness form, relaxed but deceptively alert. She twisted a lock of golden hair around her finger and grinned.

"Looks like the cat's out of the bag now, man. You may as well spill it," Taylor said with an unapologetic shrug. Russ must have told him everything, because I sure hadn't.

"Thanks, Russ. Really."

"You're welcome."

"It's us, Ian," Juni chimed in. The tiniest and quietest member of our squad gazed at me with a reassuring smile on her face. The wind kicked a few strands of dark hair into her almond shaped eyes.

"Her name's Leigh," I began after a sigh. I laid out the entire story, beginning with our chance meeting at church and ending with my decision to help her regain complete custody of her child. By the end, I'd prepared myself for laughter and merciless teasing for my gullible actions. Who gave so much money and time to a stranger they barely knew?

No one laughed.

"Well?"

Sasha shook her head. "You're a great guy, Ian. She's lucky."

"That makes you and Russ now. Funny, I always imagined ladies-man Taylor would get snagged up first." Juni passed fresh beers around the circle while Russ checked the smoked meat on the grill.

Sasha grunted and went inside. I guess she was still sore from letting go of her relationship with Taylor. We all knew why it had to happen, but it didn't ease the tender feelings on either side.

She was a lion, he was a cougar — interbreeding between our shifter species never worked out, and once the call of nature ran its course, our children were the ones to suffer most. If they survived. None of us could resist mating once we had a treasured spouse. I was already beginning to feel the tug toward Leigh, a desperate and raw urgency I denied each time we were in close proximity.

"Just you watch," Taylor said, trying to move past the awkward silence. "You'll be next, Junebug."

"Doubtful. Male rabbits are kind of pussies." Her lighthearted statement was meant to amuse us, but I heard the undercurrent of disappointment.

My phone's ringtone sang out to alert me to an incoming call then Leigh's name popped up in the caller ID window. "Hang on a sec, guys. I'll be right back."

Leaving them to laugh and make fun of male bunny shifters, I stepped aside out of shifter hearing range and answered the call. "Hi, Leigh."

"Dennis is dead. Someone stabbed him to death last night at the prison in a riot."

If anything, I'd expected to hear a heartwarming story about holding her baby again, or good news about mending the damaged relationship between her and the grandparents. She stunned me. "A prison riot? Shit. I'm sorry, hon."

"I don't even know why it's bothering me. It's not like... like we were together anymore."

"Sweetheart, it's natural to mourn him. He was a part of your life for a long while. You had a child with him."

"And now they won't let me see her," she sniffled over the line. "I mean... I sorta get why, but it's still hard, ya know? Anyway, I didn't mean to ruin your Saturday."

"You didn't ruin anything. Would you be happier if I came over?"

"No, it's all right. I'm sorry, Ian. I'm sorry."

"Stop apologizing. I did say if you ever need to talk, I'm here for you."

Leigh sniffled. "Yeah. Anyway, enjoy your Saturday, Ian. I'll see you tomorrow morning at church."

I told her goodbye and ended the call, but I

returned to the deck to find four sets of eyes watching me.

"That sounded serious," Juni spoke up tentatively. She bit her lower lip and dropped her shoulders a little. She hadn't meant to eavesdrop, but her sharp hearing picked up everything. "Are things okay?"

"Remember the ex I told you about in prison? Yeah well, somebody shanked him last night. Dead. His folks denied Leigh her scheduled visitation with her kid."

"Sounds like she needs a friend then," Russ commented. "Why are you still here?"

"She said she didn't need me to come over and would see me at church."

"Don't be daft, Ian." Sasha rolled her eyes and shook her head. "When we women tell you to stay away, we actually want you to come."

"What the fuck kind of mind game is that?" Taylor asked. "Why can't you just tell us you want us around?"

"Because then you whine about us being needy," Sasha fired back.

"Okay, okay. Before this devolves into the usual, I guess I'll head out and check on her. Sorry, guys."

"We'll be here when you get back. Not like we're driving anywhere," Taylor said. He shrugged.

"We'll hold down the fort. Here." Juni jumped up and plucked the first two steaks off the grill. We had one extra T-bone because Russ had forgotten she didn't eat meat. Within minutes, she prepared a tidy to-go package, including some of the cobbler Dani sent over with Russ.

With our meals and a bottle of merlot in my possession, I drove over to Leigh's house and knocked on the door. The neighbors watched me from their porch, filled with curiosity.

"Sup, MacArthur. Sure see you around here often. Y'all datin' now or something?" the guy asked.

Given the chance to stake my claim, I ran with it and nodded. "Yup. She's all mine now." I knocked again. "Steak delivery for Leigh Denton," I called, hoping to lure her from inside.

"Heard 'bout what happened to Dennis. Can't say it surprised me much."

"Yeah? I thought the prison system was safe these days."

"About as safe as a prison can be if you keep your mouth shut."

I didn't get a chance to inquire further. The door slowly creaked open to reveal Leigh. Her puffy face and red eyes confirmed my suspicions, proving no matter how much she claimed to be okay on the phone, she really wasn't fine at all.

"Ian? I told you not to come."

"I brought you dinner, sweetheart. You can kick me out after you take it."

After she stepped aside to let me in, I set Juni's

care package on the kitchen counter and turned around just in time to receive an armful of woman. I ran my fingers through her fair hair and eventually coaxed her to sit with me on the couch. I held her until the worst of her sobs subsided and she removed her cheek from my soaked shoulder.

"I'm s—"

"Apologize one more time and I'm gonna go and take my steaks with me."

Leigh's sniffles dwindled to weak giggles.

"When I say I'm here for you, Leigh, I mean it. You can talk as much as you want or just be quiet. It won't bother me a bit." I settled back into the couch arm and watched her. Uncertain, cloud-grey eyes studied me in return.

"I hate him so much for what he did to us," she whispered once the initial silence ended. "I used to blame him for my relapses, making up excuses all the time."

"And now you don't," I encouraged her.

Leigh nodded. "Not anymore. I spent the first month after they took Sophia thinking, 'If he didn't supply me, I could have kicked it. It's his fault.' Then I realized I was looking at it all wrong. He didn't put the pills in my mouth. I did."

In another time and place, I might have judged her too for her shitty decisions. Poor choices may have hurt her child, but the law was putting her through a mother's nightmare to get her back.

"Everything just went to hell when my dad got sick. I just feel so lost right now."

"Well, I'm pretty sure a full belly and a good movie will help a little."

With a little effort, I managed to get Leigh to eat a filling meal. The solemn mood gradually tapered off over the course of a made for TV movie. We dug into peach cobbler and took turns swigging from the merlot bottle once I assured her no one would barge in to point fingers for her decision to have a sip. A pain killer addiction didn't make her an alcoholic.

"I feel weird drinking straight out of the bottle," she murmured. "Wish I had glasses."

"It's okay, hon. There's nobody here to see us drinking like a pair of classless lushes," I reminded her. "It's only us, and I'm not telling. Unless the judge is hiding in the bushes outside your window, we're good."

Afterward, when we were both stuffed and she was clearly tipsy, she leaned against me and kissed my cheek. Her palm slipped over my chest, idly trailing up and down my torso. "Hey, Ian?"

"Hm?" God, she smelled sweet. As much as I wanted to kiss her and submit to the needs of my feral half, the man in me said to wait. Now wasn't the time to put the moves on her. Not when she was mourning and not when there was a gorgeous wine flush on her cheeks. My stiffening cock provoked a slew of lustful thoughts, imagining Leigh beneath me with her head thrown back. I wanted to feel her nails against my shoulders and tight body milking my release.

I couldn't deny my eagle much longer.

"Thanks for coming."

"It's nothin', sweetheart. Hey, instead of meeting at church tomorrow would you like to come meet some friends of mine who are in town right now?"

"You mean skip?"

"Exactly. I'm pretty sure the big man upstairs will understand, as upset as you are. You can come join us all for a big brunch since they're staying at my house tonight."

Leigh leaned back to look at me with guilt in her large, gray eyes. "Oh, Ian, you had friends over and you abandoned them to come see me? I couldn't intrude—"

"Psshaw. They'll love you. Besides, Dani will be glad to have some non-military company there. She tends to bug out and just send over treats if it's only us." I guided her back over to me with one arm around her. She came over willingly and nestled close.

"Dani?"

"Russel's girlfriend. You met him, you know, the guy who helped me out with your roof repairs."

"The big guy who looks like a bear wearing a Stetson?"

My grin widened a little. "Yeah, that one."

"Mm, he was nice. You were both so nice," she mumbled against my shoulder.

I thought I'd imagined her checking us both out when we were cooling off beneath her peach tree with our shirts off and the case of beer I fetched from the corner store. Then Russ confirmed it on the way home, and we both had a good chuckle.

Another glance down confirmed she had fallen asleep, her face closer to my neck. Without waking Leigh, I slipped my arms beneath her body and raised her up from the sofa. Her cramped bedroom was neat and tidy, with little more than a full-sized bed and a banged up dresser. Photos of her decorated the mirror in a collage style, fastened by tiny squares of tape. I tucked her in and took a moment to look at them on my way out the door.

The young woman in the high school graduation photos was at least forty pounds lighter, slim at the waist and hip. Without the cap and gown, her modest black dress revealed long legs and toned, athletic arms. Sliding my eyes back and forth between the photo and the real woman in the bed, I drew comparisons between Leigh's thicker waist, rounder face, and the picture's smaller proportions. The only thing I preferred about her younger visage was the careless smile on her face. It touched her eyes and overflowed with happiness. The Leigh I knew never smiled as freely.

After tidying up her living room, I borrowed her second bed pillow and sprawled on her new sofa. The smell of the manufacturer and showroom floor was gone, replaced by her scent. I let the memory of her touch carry me off to sleep.

5

LEIGH

I awakened without any regrets about my evening of wine sipping with Ian and spent my first conscious minute remembering the way his abs flexed beneath my stroking fingertips. The man had a stomach I wanted to kiss.

My old clock told me it was half past ten, long past the hour I usually got up to prepare for church in the morning. I groggily slipped out of bed and ran my fingers through my disheveled hair.

Just as I was preparing to set out clothes, a strange sound from my living room startled me out of the daily routine. With my dad's Louisville slugger in my hands, I tiptoed to the hall where a peek revealed Ian stretched facedown across my couch. Snoring.

I sighed.

After I spread a blanket over the chilly man, I shuffled into the bathroom and got in the shower. I made sure my legs were damned silky, wrapped a towel around myself, and stepped into the hall just in time to come face to face with Ian as he emerged from the kitchen with a glass of OJ. The kitchen doorway placed him barely two yards from me.

"Uh..." I clutched the towel a little tighter. It was tiny scrap of rectangular terry cloth insufficient for my tall frame, coming to a stop higher than mid-thigh. It barely covered my ass in the back and left an inch wide strip of my side visible. Ian's eyes followed the narrow path of ivory.

"Morning, Leigh. Hope it was okay to raid your fridge."

"Morning," I whispered back. The two yards between us became mere inches as he bridged the gap before I could shuffle into the bedroom to die of embarrassment. Beads of water glistened upon my cheeks and arms, droplets occasionally splattering against the floor from my dripping hair.

Ian moved a slick strand from my face and tucked it behind my ear. The casual gesture made me tremble with rising anticipation of the next touch. Thankfully, the plush fabric of my newer bath towel concealed how stiff my nipples hardened beneath it.

"Leigh?"

"Hm?"

"Do you have a bathing suit?"

"A b-bathing suit?" I stammered.

"It's a pool party, sweetheart."

"A pool party in November?"

"We're only a couple days into November, and it's Texas, darlin'. Sixty-five degrees out there today." His cocky, uneven grin warmed my heart. "Plus it's a heated pool."

"Oh! Just gimme a second to figure out if I have one I can still fit in."

Ian's lips brushed against my temple. "Take your time."

My favorite pre-pregnancy two-piece was a no. I didn't feel confident enough to strut my stuff in front of strangers bound to resemble the cast from Magic Mike. I settled on a blue, halter style tankini with a white polka dot print and modest boy shorts instead.

While he waited outside, I rummaged for the perfect ensemble to accentuate my curves. The sea-green pleated skirt I found suited my above average height and swished around my legs, and when paired with a wide belt to emphasize my waist, confidence surged through me as I looked in the mirror.

I emerged from my bedroom to whistles and enthused catcalls. "You look *amazing*."

"I do?" I came up short of grabbing my purse from the coffee table and stared at him.

"Pffft. As if you ever had any doubt about it."

I did, but he didn't need to know that.

~

*J*an's home was a spacious, two story nestled outside Quickdraw city limits. The massive backyard deserved its own zip code and housed an in-ground, rectangle pool with its own dive board. Sasha and Juni had stretched a volleyball net between both sides.

"C'mon, Leigh. We need one more for a game of volleyball. Ian claims you've got a badass spike," Taylor called.

"And Russ will cry if their side is short a person," Sasha added.

"I will not," Russ protested.

"He will," Dani confirmed from a lawn chair on the deck. "I'd play, but I'm feeling sort of tired from pulling those extra hours at work all week. Just gonna sit here and read a bit."

"I don't know, guys. I haven't played in a couple years." I tried to imagine myself leaping around in the water and jiggling while Sasha pranced in her white mesh bikini. The hot little number evoked instantaneous feelings of inferiority.

Then I realized they didn't care. No one gave me a cross look for my swimsuit choice.

"C'mon over to the dark side," Russ encouraged.

"Bet I can spike one past you," Ian taunted.

Fuck it. The only person who cares about my rolls is me.

Overcoming my biggest fear, I joined them in the pool and had the time of my life. The best part of all was discovering the passing of years barely dulled my skills. By the third game, it was all coming back to me in a rush. My adrenaline pumped when Ian and Russ began arguing over sharing me.

"Guys, guys. I'll swap with Sasha next game."

"But we don't want her!" Taylor cried.

The intensity of Sasha's dirty look made Taylor recoil. "Sorry. Uh, I mean... We'd love to have you, baby doll! You can have Leigh back, Ian."

We played three more games before the tough soldiers threw in the towel. Ian picked me up and swung me around in a circle, laughing because I'd won him 500 bucks off Taylor.

"Told you she had a better spike game than you," Ian taunted him.

"You brought in a ringer, man. Not cool," Taylor grumbled while the girls dragged me away to chat.

"Do you kickbox?" Juni asked.

"No, I've never tried it. Not sure it'd be so good for my knee."

"Oh." Juni flushed. "You can tell me to mind my own business if you want. I was just thinking you have great legs for it. The guy I train with has worked with people with knee injuries before, you know."

"Really?"

"Yeah." The slimmer girl beside me had a set of

muscular thighs I envied, so I couldn't imagine her believing mine were great for anything. Her modest, navy blue one-piece covered more than Sasha's bathing suit, but Juni lacked my insecurity and wore it with pride.

If I can look at her and see she looks great, why couldn't I feel the same way about myself?

"I've never really considered kickboxing before, but it could be fun once I've saved up some. I know I won't have a job with Betty forever."

Ian's glance made me regret my words. I bit my lip and ducked my head down, wishing I'd phrased it better.

"Why don't you apply to return to school?" Sasha's question pierced the tension like a knife slicing butter. I aimed an appreciative smile to her.

"I don't know. Maybe it'll be possible once Sophia is in school. I have a year of courses to finish and daycare is too pricey."

"Check and find out if any of the courses you need are available online," Dani chimed in. "I'm going to get a start on my master's and have a couple I can do from home."

By the time Russ announced the barbecue was ready, Dani had fetched a pecan pie from indoors. I ate without shame or fear of judgment, stuffing myself with delicious ribs and sweets until I slumped uselessly against Ian's chair. He slipped an arm around my shoulders, inviting me to snuggle close.

"Your friends throw good parties," I mumbled.

"The best." I may have been surrounded by hot military men, but his was the only body I wanted to cuddle.

At the end of the evening when Ian dropped me off at home, I kissed his cheek before leaving the vehicle.

"Thanks for today."

"Looks like they all loved you, sweetheart."

"I loved meeting them too."

It was a struggle to unwind for bed after a day with Ian's amazing, nonjudgmental friends. With only hours to go before between me and the biggest day of my entire life, I sipped chamomile tea to soothe my nerves. Sophia and Ian's faces blessed my dreams once I finally fell into slumber.

~

*M*y custody hearing should have been an open and shut case. It started with Judge Ritts asking for my proof of employment, which I provided when I passed over my pay stubs.

"How do you plan to continue working once Sophia is in your care, Ms. Denton?"

"I have an agreement with my boss and client. Sophia will come to work with me each day."

"That isn't very professional. A child in a working environment?"

"They've both encouraged it. I brought a written statement from her and my employer." I slid those to him. Ritts set both aside when he finished reading then he sighed.

"I received a report from child protective services about the state of your home. I couldn't in good faith allow her to return to you until I've received proof it's hazard free."

Thanks to Ian's advice, I came prepared with a few Polaroids. I set those in front of the judge, too, and watched him exchange a dubious glance with Sophia's grandparents.

Everything seemed to lean in my favor, pending another drug screening and a home assessment by CPS. Then Mr. and Mrs. James had their lawyer drop a bombshell on me.

They wanted to retain custody of my little girl and claimed they would give her the life I never could. When the judge asked me if I would voluntarily surrender my parental rights, it took every ounce of my control to decline without profanity. I glanced behind me to see Ian staring daggers at the judge, his jaw clenched. He was angry, but I couldn't breathe. All of the air was leached from my lungs, my emotional pain manifesting as physical agony I'd never felt before.

Judge Ritts demanded more proof I could provide a

stable home. Apparently my employment, growing bank account, and sobriety didn't count. We would reconvene in a month to decide the fate of my parental privileges. I left the courtroom feeling numb from head to toe, barely aware of my surroundings or that Ian was guiding me to his Escalade by one arm. My foggy head made it difficult to focus, and I stumbled going down the steps. Ian steadied me.

"Hey, I've got you. Slow down, Leigh."

"I've done everything. Everything they asked," I whispered. My body was numb, useless as he guided me.

"The Good Ol' Boy System at work," Ian muttered. He shook his head and opened my car door.

Despite Dennis' crimes, his mother and father were still highly respected in the community. As far as our fellow residents believed, his wrongdoing wasn't because they'd spared the rod and spoiled the child — it was me, the junkie and corruptor who led him down his wayward path. I had the drug history and criminal background he didn't have prior to his arrest. Dennis got caught up in my bullshit, and now he was dead at the young age of twenty-five, his light extinguished too soon.

"What do I do now, Ian?"

"We'll fight it. My friend, Argus, specializes in finances, but I'll ask him if he can recommend an associate in family law. I should have gotten you a lawyer to begin with."

"I can't afford a lawyer."

"*I* will pay for it."

"And I can't ask for you to do it!"

"You're not asking me, but I'm telling you this will happen, and you'll owe me nothing for it. Because it's the right thing to do, and I wouldn't be able to sleep at night if I don't."

"There has to be a way to do this without costing you a lot of money."

Ian rubbed his chin thoughtfully and gazed into the distance. "I'll have a word with them. We can try conversation first. I'll talk it out with Mr. James, and we can do this like men."

"It's not going to be easy, Ian. You can't just strut into someone's house and lay down the law like you're back in the Arm—"

"Air Force," he corrected me.

"Air Force," I gritted out through my teeth. "They don't have any reason to believe a single word you say to them. They don't have a reason to trust *me*. What? Do you think I haven't tried to get through to them?"

"I understand, Leigh."

The thing I hated about Ian was no matter how much I ranted and raged, he kept a cool head and waited it out as I transitioned from despair to fury.

"The hell you do!" My sharp scream startled me,

but it failed to coax a reaction out of him. "What do you know except that your current charity case is about to lose her daughter for good? Why do you even care? You don't have anything to gain from this. Why are you here at all?"

"Are you done?" he asked gently.

Sniffling, I wiped my eyes with his handkerchief and nodded. Crying was exhausting business.

"Good. You want to know why I care so much, so I'll tell you, Leigh. I care because after my dad died, *my* mom gave me up. She didn't want me. When Gramps passed away, it was just Grams and me and a lot of people didn't think she could raise a little boy alone. Maybe she didn't make your mistakes, but she did right by me. I believe you mean it when you swear you're off the drugs."

The story of Ian's family history jarred me out of my self-pity session. I stared at him through the haze of my tears. "She gave you up?"

"Yeah. I was about to celebrate my sixth birthday. She walked out of my life and didn't try to contact me until she heard I had a big military commission. Tried to write her son the Colonel, and she made sure to ask me for money, too."

I couldn't imagine walking away from a child without a damned good reason for doing it.

"Did she ever tell you why?"

"Yeah, she did." Ian's pained smile told me everything I needed to know. I didn't pry. "Anyway, why don't we go and have lunch to give them a chance to return home."

"They won't listen to you, Ian."

"They will. Trust me. When I finish with what I have to say, they'll be glad to give Sophia back to you."

6

IAN

I knocked on the door to the James household without a single plan in my head. I knew they loved the kid, but what they had decided to do went above and beyond the call of justice. They were trying to replace their child with someone else's daughter.

Leigh made her mistakes, but she'd received her punishments and fulfilled every stipulation set by the law. So why hadn't the judge restored custody at the hearing? I had my guesses.

Someone peeked at me through the peephole then I heard the rustling of a security chain. As the door cracked open, I assumed my most unintimidating stance, with my hands folded together behind my back and my spine straight.

The portly older man in the doorway smiled at me,

no doubt aware of the reason for my visit. "Mr. MacArthur, what can we do for you?"

"I'd like to talk to you about Leigh and Sophia. May I come in?"

Mr. James stiffened and clenched his jaw. "I think we've spoken enough about Leigh and Sophia."

The whole town knew I served in the military. I had a reputation here, and I certainly didn't plan to fuck it up by scaring an old man in his own home. I wanted to chat with him on the level, but he was making it hard to remain patient when I couldn't even get a foot in the door.

"You haven't talked with me personally on the matter," I said quietly. "You can let me in now, or you can wait until I contact a lawyer. Which will it be?"

"Lawyer" was the magic word. The old man let me in this time, and we took seats in the living room, him in his chair and me on the sofa.

"I'm sorry about your son, but I'm going to cut straight to the point, Mr. James. None of you have any reason at all to suspect Leigh hasn't turned over a new leaf. She's clean. She's passed every piss test the state has thrown at her. She's working—"

"At a job you created for her," the man cut in.

"A job is a job," I replied mildly. "This recent request is a slap to the face. Don't you think it's been long enough? A child deserves to have a mother. Leigh loves Sophia. She'd do anything for her — has done everything for her. She's been clean almost four months."

"And when she relapses, then what? Sophia's gonna be the one to suffer."

"She won't."

"You don't know that," he insisted while rocking in his chair.

"You can't punish her for something she hasn't done yet, either."

"She is my grandbaby. I'm not going to let her mom ruin her life, not when we can give her better."

The way they gave Dennis better? I bit back the retort and kept the irritation from my expression and my voice. "Sophia will have a great home. With her mom."

"In that ramshackle drug den of hers? No, Mr. MacArthur, I don't think so."

"No. In *my* home. I plan to marry Leigh. We're on our way to the city hall now for the marriage license," I spit out. My temper got the best of me and took charge, sweeping me down a road I couldn't reverse. "I'm going to marry her and adopt Sophia. So you can listen to me now and back off, or wait to see the both of us in court. I promise you, it's going to be costly, and you won't like the outcome if we take the legal route."

I knew he had Judge Ritts in his pocket, and their fishing buddy friendship was the reason Leigh couldn't get a fair shot. What Mr. James and Judge Ritts didn't know was one fucking phone call from me would have him removed by morning. I was willing to take a chance and call in a favor.

~

"What do you mean we're getting married?"

"I kind of lost my temper and said I plan to marry you. Then I said we'll see them in court."

For my safety, I decided to lay the news on Leigh after we were on the road and driving toward the next town.

"Where are we going?" Leigh demanded.

"To buy a marriage license."

"Fuck no. I'm not marrying you."

"Well, you might want to listen to the rest of what I have to say before you make up your mind."

Leigh settled back in her seat and fixed me with a scowl so dark it could curdle milk. I winced and turned my attention back to the road. "I'm waiting."

"If I'm married to you, I have the legal right to stand beside you in court. And just between you and me, I have a military history, no criminal record, and enough money to buy half this town. Alternatively, I can also pull a lot of strings to get Judge Ritts disbarred. What he did today was a severe miscarriage of our justice system, and I'll be damned if I allow him to get away with it. You met their requirements."

"I don't know, Ian. He's been a judge for forty years. He's not a bad man. It'll ruin him and drag his name through the mud."

"But he's discriminating against you," I pointed out.

"I know but—"

"Do you want Sophia back?"

Leigh silenced. With her eyes on the window, a thoughtful expression came over her pretty face. She'd made mistakes, but the James' decisions would follow her for a lifetime. "I want my baby, Ian."

"Marry me, Leigh. I have a big house you and Sophia are welcomed to share with me."

"What about..." She cleared her throat and gestured between us. "I mean, we haven't even had a first date. Not really. Marriage is..."

"It's convenient for both of us. In a year or so, after you finish school, we can have it annulled or divorce to go our separate ways. I'll make sure you're comfortable." Like hell we would. My deepest hope was she'd come to feel for me what I felt for her.

"So that's it? A fake marriage and I get to live in a big house?"

"Did you expect more?" I took a shot in the dark and stole a look at her from the corner of my eye. "Some kind of perverted sex stipulation?"

Hot color spread over her face. Bingo.

"Sex is a very personal, intimate thing for me, Leigh. It goes against my principles to expect you to lay down with me just because I'm giving you a hand."

Maybe it had something to do with my shifter half. Eagles mated for life, and the few times I'd have had sex with a woman simply to satisfy a craving, the lack of attachment made me feel empty inside. Incomplete. It was an impression I couldn't shake, too intense to risk repeating unnecessarily.

"It's personal for me, too," Leigh confided.

"I meant what I said about taking you out and getting to know you better, Leigh. Look, my house is big enough for you to have your own bedroom. We'll take it slow and see how things develop."

"What if I don't want to marry you?"

"Then I'll find you the best lawyer I can retain on short notice and we'll take this to court."

"What if I marry you and it gets awkward?"

"Then in a year, they'll see you haven't relapsed and we can split." The idea had its charm and gave me a year to show her I could be the man she wanted for the rest of her life.

"Okay."

"Okay what?"

"I'll marry you."

"Church or courthouse?" I glanced over at her and grinned. Leigh wiped the tears from her face with one hand and grinned back at me.

"Courthouse. Think I've had enough of church for a while."

~

"Wait, wait, what?" Russ choked on his beer until his girlfriend slapped him on the back.

"I said I need a best man. A witness. Whatever it is."

"You're joking, right?"

Dani swatted Russ. "I don't see him laughing, hon. Of course we'll come, Ian."

"Thanks, Daniela, it means a lot to me."

"Hold on a minute now. Don't you think you're rushing into this? Have you talked to her or told her *why* you feel so strongly about her already?" Russ asked.

Daniela rolled her eyes. "Don't listen to the bear stalker over here. If there's one thing I've learned about you strange shifters, it's that your hearts lead you to the right place."

Abashed, Russ exhaled a low sigh. "Sorry. I guess she's right, but are you sure this is what you want to do?"

"I had all night to think about it, Russ. We were supposed to have our first official date yesterday, but after we bought a marriage license at the county courthouse, I spent the evening letting her cry on my shoulder instead," I said.

"What I don't get is why it's taken so long for Ian to find his fated mate," Dani mused.

"There could be any number of reasons, darlin'. Could be he wasn't truly ready to settle down," Russ explained.

I nodded in confirmation. "Have you ever heard the saying 'there's someone for everyone'? It really should be 'there's a few people for everyone' because as our life circumstances change..."

"So do the people we're destined to find," Russ said. "Katie was always the woman for me, but her death made room for you, Dani. You were my other soul mate, the one I never knew I had. Because I'd bonded once in my life, it took a while for me to realize you and I bonded."

"You guys make it sound so romantic. It would make a beautiful movie plot line, I bet. A tale of a man searching his whole life for his other half, only to find her where he least expects her."

"Yeah, in a church of all places," I grunted.

"My dad used to say church was the best place to find 'em," Russ commented.

"I guess that's why Dani found your lazy ass in her yard like some hairy sleeping beauty instead of down the road at the Methodist church around the corner."

Russ grunted this time. "Anyway, back to your

problem. We'll be there. Just let us know if you need anything else, like help moving her things."

Where would I be without the support of my friends? "Nah. We're going to start tomorrow."

We waited two days instead, taking Wednesday as a cooling off time away from each other to decide what was best. While waiting, I contacted Argus and placed my thumb on a couple contacts who owed me favors. I prepared for the worst possible outcome, which was Leigh deciding she wanted me to go after Judge Ritts. Alternatively, if she wanted to fight, a fancy lawyer from San Antonio was waiting to come to the rescue. The man was so good my pal Argus claimed by the time he finished our defense, Sophia would be back in Leigh's care and her grandparents would be paying child support.

Leigh didn't want that either.

By Thursday, I drove up in my Escalade to find her wrapping photo frames and small keepsakes. Russ planned to visit later in the evening to fetch her couch with his pickup. It was too new to leave behind like the bed.

I waited until the next day, after she was long gone and clear of reprisal before calling the police department about her dealing neighbors. While Leigh unpacked some of her clothes into her new bedroom, I snuck away into my office and got on the line to the Quickdraw Police Department.

"We're aware of some problems from that house, Mr. MacArthur," the young woman said. She didn't sound like an officer and had to be one of the girls in the office since I knew we had an all-male force.

"Excuse me?" I asked. "If your officers are aware of it, why aren't they doing anything?"

"I can't answer those questions over the—"

"I'd like to speak to the chief." She put me through a ten minute wait before Montgomery answered the line.

"What can I do for you, Mr. MacArthur?"

"There are people openly dealing drugs down on Denning Street and you aren't doing anything about it?"

"We've gotten calls, Mr. MacArthur, nothing else. There's no proof of wrongdoing there."

"That's bullshit, Montgomery, and you know it. I sat outside Leigh's house fifteen minutes the other day and saw everything I needed to know. They've even got the little kid rushing down the steps to peddle their dope because they're too lazy to get off their asses." Leigh had a card from her CPS caseworker, and while I hated to get any parent into trouble with the law, my conscience wouldn't allow it to rest. I had to call.

"Now hold on a minute, Ian."

"Oh, now we're on a first name basis, are we? My fiancée is out of that house now, but I want to know what you plan to do about it. I can drive through north side at any hour of the day and catch a handful of drug deals going down by the Dixie Quarters. Why is this happening?"

"There are things happening behind the scenes that I can't discuss," Montgomery said. His snide tone made me wish I could strangle him over the line. "Sometimes, it's to our benefit to allow some small fish to go free until we catch the keepers, if you get my drift."

"*Some* small fish to go free? It's become very apparent that Quickdraw has a 100% catch and release program in effect," I said dryly.

Montgomery silenced. I pictured him fuming in his office and grinned. "I won't discuss police matters over the line, MacArthur. I can only tell you to take comfort in knowing we've got it under control."

"Thanks for your time." I ended the call and glanced up to see Leigh in the doorway, frowning.

"Is everything okay, Ian?"

"Oh, everything's great. Nothing I can't handle," I said. She didn't need to be bothered any more on the matter. "Did you get Petunia settled in yet?"

"Oh yeah. She loves it here. Those puppies ought to be here any day now, too."

Richard and Gloria James showed up at my home the following afternoon as we were unloading cleaning supplies from our final trip out to her old house. Everything was ready to go on the market.

"I'm going inside," Leigh murmured to me. As she stepped toward the door, I grabbed her by the wrist and anchored her in place.

"You don't have to run from anyone, Leigh."

The elderly couple picked their way down the drive. Gloria walked with a cane these days, following a recent knee replacement surgery. Her husband was a brittle diabetic and just as poor in health. Their son, prior to his arrest for drug crimes, had been their sole caretaker.

I had to wonder how either of them thought they could take care of a child. If not for a crooked judge, they wouldn't have had a chance.

"Hello, Mr. MacArthur. This isn't a bad time, is it?"

"No. We're just finishing up. What can I do for you?"

"We wanted to apologize to Leigh for what's happened. Your visit gave us a chance to talk and come to our senses. Thank you, young man."

I was hardly as young as I appeared. The magic flowing through my veins slowed aging. We didn't live more than a decade or two longer than most humans, but we looked better during our lifetimes. So did our bonded mates.

"We don't want to take it to court, now that we know you'll be here to help Leigh. I... we can't use Sophia to replace Dennis. He's gone now. There's no bringing him back, and he made his decisions," Gloria said.

"Where's Leigh so we can tell her in person?" Richard asked.

Leigh stepped out from behind my vehicle. "I'm right here."

"Leigh, we're sorry. We were so carried away with our pain. And after Dennis died, we just lost sight of what was best for Sophia. He wouldn't have wanted this. He wouldn't have wanted all of us fighting this way."

I glanced at the open backseat and saw a rear-facing child seat. Sophia was with them of course, her wide-eyed features alert and aware of her surroundings.

"Do you mean I can see her now? Right now?"

The older man nodded. Without another word, Leigh dashed for the car and slid in beside Sophia. I watched with a smile on my face.

"You did the right thing," I told them both as Leigh reconnected with her daughter. Those sporadic, monitored visits to their home hadn't been enough.

"We made contact with the social worker. We can't leave her here with Leigh just yet, not legally, but you're both welcome in our home at any time until we hear back from Mrs. Johnson."

"Thank you, Mrs. James. Have you set a date and time for Dennis' funeral?"

The older woman nodded. They only had about a decade on me, but the vast differences in our appearance came as a benefit of my shifter traits and healthier lifestyle. "We plan to put him to rest Saturday afternoon. We'd like it if both of you came."

"Of course." I hoped Leigh didn't disapprove of my agreement.

I invited the couple inside my home for coffee while Leigh bonded with her child in the living room. We gave her complete freedom from our prying eyes and stayed clear. She didn't need a monitor. She wouldn't harm Sophia.

"Cream, sugar?" I asked. A little friendly interaction went a long way, and despite the minor difference in our ages, I treated them with the same respect I'd give my gram.

"Yes, please," Gloria answered.

"If you don't mind my asking, Mr. MacArthur, how old are you?"

"Ian, please. And no, I don't mind. I actually get this a lot. I'll be fifty-four next month."

Their eyes bugged. I've heard every kind of joke, from having great genes to having the same physical fitness trainer as Brad Pitt. I didn't look my age and I never would.

"Well, you sure don't show it," Gloria commented.

A sweet soprano drifted from the living room into

the kitchen. The lullaby was a familiar tune, but I'd never found it particularly pretty until now.

"Is that Leigh?"

"It is. You didn't know she could sing?"

"She never talks about singing. She only told me she likes to hear the choir at church." We had talked about volleyball, her sports injuries, and her failure to complete college, but singing never made the conversation. She had a beautiful voice.

"Leigh used to be the best in the choir before..." Richard's voice trailed.

It became crystal for me then, and I was able to understand everything about the sorrow on her face during the service. I finally knew her reasons for attending despite their unwelcoming behavior.

"Would they let her in the choir again now? Look, I know you don't much like her the way you used to, but even you have to admit she's paid her dues. What do we have to do to get this town to accept it?"

They looked at each other. "I think everything has to start with us, Ian."

*M*y husband-to-be arrived in jeans. He wore them well, but I couldn't help but mourn the loss of the classic fairy tale wedding from my childhood fantasies.

In my dreams, I'd wear an exquisite white gown with trailing lace while a half dozen bridesmaids beamed proudly from beside the altar. They wore blue, my favorite color, with wine-colored sashes around their waists. I had flowers in my hair and a piano player skillfully announcing my arrival with the wedding march. His hands would glide over the ivories and I'd emerge to find a captive audience who melted before my beauty on my special day. My father would lead me down the aisle to a handsome man in a flaw-less tuxedo, join our hands, and give me away with tears in his eyes.

The crushing reality was a Wal-Mart dress from the clearance aisle and two of Ian's friends in their Sunday best. My dad died two years ago from throat cancer and my friends scattered like cockroaches when the shit hit the fan after Sophia's birth.

One glance at the man beside me sped my pulse rate to a jackhammer pace. Ian was a good-looking man, a kind man, and there were worse guys to marry. I'd hoped his kindness would soothe the butterflies in my belly, but it didn't. I nervously smoothed my fingers over the edge of my yellow and white sundress.

"It's not too late to change your mind," Ian whispered in my ear.

"I should be telling you that." It was his crazy idea, after all.

"Nah, I'm good."

The simple ceremony lacked fanfare. An old tape player running in the background provided our Wedding March and the magistrate stood by a long table where our wedding license waited. He spoke a few solemn words regarding the sanctity of marriage before asking if we each accepted the other. Then he had us sign the papers. Envying Ian's steady handwriting, I tried to script my own name without my pen shaking all over the line. He was unwavering, steel nerves and perfect composure.

"I now pronounce you husband and wife. You may kiss your bride."

Instinctively, my eyes shifted from the judge to my new husband and found Ian closely watching me in return. Before I could concoct a phony excuse or claim modesty, Ian's mouth lowered against mine.

Ian swept me away with his intensity. My fingers threaded through his silvering hair and anchored him in place as surely as the arms around my waist held me to his military-honed physique. Years after his retirement, he was still built like a soldier at the peak of his career.

His tongue darted between my lips, prompting me to open my mouth in acceptance. My nipples tightened beneath my strapless bra and our audience vanished from my memory. Only the tangle of our tongues mattered, along with how much I wanted to guide Ian's hand from my waist to my breasts, or better yet, to place it between my thighs where my panties dampened.

I came away from the kiss breathless and red-cheeked, the heat spreading all the way to the neckline of my dress like a badge of embarrassment for everyone to see. From the corner of my vision, I caught sight of Ian's strange champagne-colored eyes with a smirk on his face, watching me.

Seconds after we exited the courtroom, I twisted to whisper in his ear, "Did you really have to kiss me that way in front of everyone?" To keep from meeting his gaze, I smoothed the skirt of my dress and picked at a minute speck of lint.

"We certainly won't have to worry about anyone questioning the validity of our marriage now, will we?" he countered.

"Point."

"Photo time," Dani called out.

I liked Russ and Dani. They were the perfect couple, polar opposites in appearance and completely adorable. I envied her confidence as much as I was jealous of her big breasts. She'd lucked out in the curvaceous figure department with striking, proportionate measurements all around.

"You both look so cute together," Betty said.

"I—we do?" I asked, startled.

"My dear, you are always beautiful, but even my failing eyes can see you and my grandson look marvelous together."

Betty remained clueless. I had to wonder if his plan was for her benefit as much as it was to help me. At her age, she didn't have much longer to see her grandson happily married, and in a way, this made Sophia her great-granddaughter.

Prior to the wedding, I'd signed something drawn up by Ian's lawyer and faxed to us, forfeiting any and all rights to his pension, properties, and holdings. I didn't want those, and even if I did, how much of a bitch would I look for trying to steal a veteran's hard-earned savings?

At the end of the evening, after a restaurant dinner with Russ, Dani, and Betty, we all went our separate ways. I hugged Dani and Russ in the parking lot outside the restaurant then Ian and I drove Betty home.

By the time Ian had pulled into his driveway, I could barely breathe. My vision swam a little as I crossed the threshold into my new home.

"What's wrong?" Ian asked.

"Nothing. It's still hard for me to believe your living room is as big as my whole house," I confessed. The whole floor plan of my former home could be shoved into the room he dedicated to his big screen television and social furnishings. The bedrooms were as generous, providing more space than I even needed.

Ian's personal bathroom had a shower worthy of my dreams. I'd nearly chosen the downstairs bedroom by the kitchen for its personal bathroom, until Ian coaxed me to check out the entire house. I didn't regret it. It was worth sharing a restroom with the man for the umbrella shaped shower fixture. I soaked beneath it for a half hour, enjoying the luxurious spray, unrushed and without fear of the water heater crapping out.

I found Ian on the couch with his laptop and a beer in front of a movie. According to Betty, he liked to watch action flicks for background noise while working on government projects.

"Hey, finally settled?"

"I think so," I replied. Taking the seat beside him, I nestled into the couch corner and brushed out my damp hair while he fetched me a beer and snacks, too.

Some wedding night. Bride and groom retire to their honeymoon to chastely watch Liam Neeson films all night with bowls of popcorn and a goodie bag from their friends.

A wicked part of me wanted to test the boundaries of our new marriage by offering my body. I had trouble reconciling that he came into this deal without expectations of benefitting from our arrangement.

I mulled it over until the credits rolled an hour later.

"Well, I'm going to bed. G'night, Leigh."

"Night, Ian."

And then my chance was gone. The whole town probably thought we were wrapped naked around each other by now.

I stole a peek at his retreating shape when he left the room. Ian was an excellent example of a man for his age. I still couldn't believe he was fifty-three. Hell, I hadn't wanted to believe he was out of his thirties yet. He must have belonged to the same vampire club as Brad Pitt, Johnny Depp, and Keanu Reeves. In each of his pictures — there were many framed photographs of him receiving some medal or another — he looked exactly the same except touches of silver in his dark hair grew more prominent over the years.

My own personal Dorian Grey, unaging and beautiful.

"If you need anything, you know where to find me," he called back from the stairs.

"Okay."

I remained on the sofa long after Ian left, feeling cold and numb all the way to the tips of my toes. The day's events instilled a surreal sense of disbelief, and I found myself waiting to awaken from the dream.

To prepare myself for the difficult day ahead of me, I set my alarm for an ungodly hour and lay down in my bed to sleep. It wasn't like the neighborhood where I'd lived, where the gangbangers drove their cars at all hours of the night, bass thumping from their trunks. The silence unnerved me and made it difficult to sleep.

When I awakened in the unfamiliar bedroom, my eyes blinked open to gradually adjust to the shaded interior. There weren't any water stains or cracks in the ceiling, and no fear of the roaches crawling over me in my sleep. This was home, and I had every reason to be grateful to my savior.

Once I made the bed and parted the blackout curtains, I washed my face and shuffled into the kitchen to find Ian had beat me to the punch. I'd thought I would surprise him with bacon and eggs, but

I found the man in his flannel pants with a mixing bowl of pancake batter.

"Well shit," I muttered. "How are you awake already?"

He twisted around to look at me and grinned. "The early bird gets the worm."

"Uh huh."

"How'd you sleep?"

"Lousy," I answered honestly. I plucked a banana from the fruit bowl and busied myself with peeling it to avoid prolonged eye contact with the sexy soldier at the stove. His navy blue tee clung to him so snugly he may as well have gone without it. I could see every muscle through the tightly stretched cotton. I wanted to *touch* every muscle, too.

"Do you mind if I make coffee," I asked.

"Coffee sounds great. There should be some ground beans left in the fridge, and the maker is at the end of the counter in the bottom cabinet."

Leftovers made up the bulk of his food stock, as well as a near empty gallon of milk, bottled beer, and a sack of apples. I found the coffee beans behind an unopened ketchup bottle in the door compartment.

"What is going on with this kitchen?" I finally demanded.

"Huh?"

I don't know what came over me, but I began removing things from cabinets and setting them on the counter. The man's kitchen was a disorganized mess of misplaced goods I began tidying on a whim.

"Needs a spice rack."

My confused new roomie turned to look at me. His brows raised.

"I mean, nothing in here makes sense. There's no flow," I said.

All of his pots and pans were at the opposite end of the kitchen away from the stove, and cooking utensils were scattered across several drawers, as if he tossed them in whichever was closest to hand at the time. I discovered pantry items in cabinets with the bowls or tucked away wherever there was room.

"Peanut butter with the plates," I muttered in disbelief.

"That bad, huh?"

My hand froze on the offensive sandwich spread jar. "I'm sorry," I blurted out right away. "I didn't mean to be bitchy or seem like I don't appreciate what you're doing for me, 'cause I do. I just thought—"

"Nah, it's okay. It's your kitchen too, now." Grinning the whole while, Ian gave me this boyish, heart-melting shrug like I'd embarrassed him. It was the one time when his crow's feet showed, and even then, they were only a few faint lines at the corners of his eyes.

He served me a breakfast of chocolate chip pancakes and maple syrup, but the irregular size of the chocolate pieces led me to think he'd broken up a candy bar. A glance at the wrapper in the trash confirmed my theory.

"You went out of your way for me," I said in a conversational tone once my plate was clean. He moved to rise, so I leapt from the chair to beat him to the punch, collecting the empty plates from the table. He chuckled and offered me the last sausage link from his plate. I was too ravenous to turn it down.

"I want you to feel comfortable here," he pointed out as he helped load the dishwasher, or at least tried to. My competitive spirit forced me to hip bump him out of my way. "Feel free to change anything else you'd like if it'll make you feel comfortable. There's going to be social workers in and out of this place for a while, I guess, so." He leaned against the counter, fixing his pale eyes on me. "It needs to feel like a home and not a bachelor pigsty."

"It's not a pigsty," I blurted, quickly jumping to his defense.

"It's not exactly a place for a baby either. We can remedy that after the weekend when you're up for it. I'll withdraw some cash for now, but Monday I'll call my banker up and get a monthly allowance deposited into an extra account for you."

With the dishwasher filled, I returned to rearranging the clean plates and plastic cups. I'd expected a rich bachelor like him to live like a movie star inside his home not a frat boy in his first apartment. "Allowance?"

"I'll start you off with a couple grand to spend on this place. After that we need... you need to get some more clothes. Appropriate clothes," he muttered, seeming to speak to himself more than he was talking to me.

"What's wrong with my clothes?"

"You wear them till they're worn thin, sweetie," he pointed out, gentle as ever and aware of my embarrassment. "Look, your sleeve has a hole at the elbow."

Heat crept up my neck and into my cheeks, but I wasn't sure if it was caused by his words or because he'd moved in close. His hands smoothed up my arms, over the threadbare sleeves of my shirt.

I wanted to kiss him. I wanted him to grab me like he did in front of the judge and prove our marriage wasn't a mere convenience or act of benevolence. Most of all, I wanted to forget my ex-boyfriend and the father of my child would be put to rest in the town cemetery, closing the worst chapter of my life for good.

"You should pick Sophia out some pretty new clothes, too. Monday, we'll stop by Social Security to get your name changed then the DMV for your driver's license update."

"Ian?"

"Hm?"

One step forward placed me in his personal space,

allowing me to loop one arm around his shoulders. I didn't need to stand on tiptoe since we were almost the same height.

"Thank you."

Before my nerves failed me, I leaned in and slanted my mouth over his. Ian's firm lips parted at the questing sweep from my tongue, and the next moments were dedicated to shared exploration rather than a forceful invasion. Our kiss was unbridled passion and longing, a hunger nurtured by weeks of mutual attraction rather than a sudden flash of lust. Orange juice flavored his tongue, the perfect accompaniment to the sweetness of feeling his mouth against mine.

I learned more about Ian MacArthur in the thirty seconds of our embrace than I did since our meeting on my doorstep. He became more frenzied, desperate, dragging me in by a hand molded to my ass. The close quarters exposed me to his erection, stiff and unyielding where we trapped it between our bodies, prompting me to wiggle just enough to stir a moan out of him. It was an empowering change of pace from the way I usually felt about myself.

Ian did find me attractive. He did want me, and maybe I wasn't fooling myself if I dreamed of a future with him beyond our agreement.

His sigh clenched my belly as he squeezed my ass one last time. "We better get ready for the funeral. I told the Jameses we'd be there early to help out at the wake."

Are we not going to talk about sucking face in your kitchen? His cavalier attitude sort of peeved me until I looked down and saw a hard-on tenting his pants.

"Right. I'll just go get ready then." And take care of the ache between my thighs while I was at it. Living with a sexy man was going to be its own sort of trial until we figured out where to take our marriage.

8

IAN

I don't know what came over Leigh, but I liked it and wished I'd handled the aftermath with more dignity. We dressed in our funeral attire and made the drive to the James residence before noon, where the bustling household had filled with mourners. Cars filled the street, parked up and down the block on both sides of the road. We had to park at the corner and walk back.

"What if everyone looks at me crazy?" Leigh asked.

"We'll do it back to them. I'll have you know my experience as a military officer grants me the ability to pull off insane very well."

Her giggle warmed my spirit, and in return, I tried to give her the strength to make it through her day. We ascended the walking path to the front door hand in hand, putting on a front as a happy, newlywed couple.

Leigh squeezed my fingers until my hand tingled from the loss of circulation.

The entire house silenced, save for Sophia's fussy squalling. I felt like a character in an awkward romantic comedy, waiting for the punch line to the joke or for the audience to laugh. All eyes turned to us and while a pervading sense of tension made me regret the offer to arrive early to provide support.

"Leigh! Ian, thank you for coming." Gloria limped to us with Sophia cradled on her right side, only to pass the infant to me and throw her arms around Leigh. She was the very model of acceptance and love, startling me as much as my wife.

My wife. The strange reality of it hadn't yet sunk in until I held her child against me. Sophia had ceased fussing almost immediately. Held securely in my arms, she looked up at me with curiosity and waved her chubby little fists.

I offered to drive to the cemetery and the Jameses accepted with grace and gratitude. To my surprise, the small and tasteful service was well attended as if Dennis James hadn't been a petty thug and drug dealer. Maybe he had been more at one point in his life, but I had trouble seeing beyond the mess he left behind.

Thank you, I thought. *Thank you for leaving me this wonderful woman and beautiful child.*

With Sophia in her lap, Leigh sat beside Gloria and

held the woman's hand while I stood behind them resting my hands on Leigh's shoulders. When the coffin was lowered and the service was over, we returned to the James residence for a repast with the close friends and family.

"Hold Sophia for me, Ian?" Leigh asked me.

"Sure. Pass her over."

While Leigh helped in the kitchen, I walked Sophia around and tried to socialize with mourners.

"Hello, Mr. MacArthur. I guess the new marriage means you'll be in town for a time, eh?"

I turned around to face a graying man ten years my senior. I smiled at the old war veteran. "I told you last time we talked, Ian's fine. And yeah, I suppose I'll be around for a good while now. I usually only take a few government contracts a year, if I can help it."

I knew Henry Banks from taking my grandmother to bingo at the VFW Hall a few times a month. When I wasn't around, he often did it.

"How's Betty?"

"She's doing well. Why don't you stop by and see her?" I encouraged him.

As we lapsed into talk about my grandmother, a crowd of ladies surrounded me to see the deceased's daughter. She was passed from arm to arm and loved by many.

"She's going to have his eyes," one woman said with admiration as she passed the baby back to me. I had no idea where she drew that conclusion. Sophia had Leigh's eyes without a chance of them being brown.

"I suppose we'll see soon enough," I replied, neutral and cordial all at once.

We blew off church the next day since Gram was feeling under the weather. Leigh and I checked in on her for a time, and then on Monday, I coerced my wife to take my Escalade to town for a shopping trip and to fetch groceries for Gram. While she was gone, I walked the half mile to Russ' house at the end of the dirt road. A long time ago, when I was barely an adult, I'd built the cabin to be close to Gram when she denied my request to move in with her after boot camp.

A young man needed his space, she'd said. Years later, when loneliness drove her to move closer to town to be in the community, she gave my childhood home to me and told me to do as I pleased.

So I rented it out to Daniela Reyes, and in doing so, introduced her to the love of her life and my best friend.

Russ passed me off another bottle of Shiner while Dani tended the grill for a reversal of roles. Watching my pal's mate flounder as he called out suggestions was better than most television shows.

"So, what's the latest news? I've missed a lot between the wedding and the funeral."

"Well, Dani was down at the feed store fetching some oats for Daisy when she overheard a couple of the guys gossiping on the sidewalk over a game of checkers. They're saying drug problems out in town are worse than ever."

"It's true. I had a flight over town a month ago and saw all kinds of crap. Mostly weed and small time dealing. What did she hear?" I brought the cool beer to my lips for a swig and listened. As a consistent resident for the past three years, Russ knew more about the local community than I did.

"Crack. Methamphetamine. Apparently drug dealers are cooking meth out in the boondocks. I'm pretty sure I caught a whiff of something the other day, too."

"Out here?" I jerked up straight in my seat and stared at him. "Aw shit. Here I thought it was limited to a bunch of kids dealing weed or prescription pharm they stole from their grandparents."

"Well, they've graduated to making meth labs in shacks," Russ said bluntly.

I grimaced. His news robbed me of the taste for my beer.

"Are the police doing anything about it?"

"They're a five-man police force, Ian. What do you think?"

"Six if you include Chief Montgomery. Not enough to take down a drug ring on their own." Ideas manifested in my head.

"Oh no. No, no, no, man. I know that look on your

face. I know when you're up to no good. We're not a two-man SWAT team. We're not police investigators or whatever you'd call the drug folk—"

"The DEA," I chipped in to be helpful. Russell growled and shot a dirty look at me.

"Either way, we're not them. We're military operatives currently enjoying some relaxation from our last job fighting insurgents."

"You live here too, Russ. You think Dani wants to pick up and leave?"

"I really don't," Dani called from the grill.

Russ' consternation failed to wipe the smug look off my face. I knew I had him from the moment his girlfriend stepped over to join us and turned her brown eyes his way.

"Russ, I love living out here. Remember the murder in town we heard about a month ago? It was drug related. Safety and security is the whole reason people move to small towns like this. We leave the cities like Houston behind to be *safe*." Dani shivered. She kept a couple guns of her own in their house, and boy did she know how to use them, but it didn't change that our peaceful community had transformed.

"Fine. I'll do some sniffing around when I'm in town too," the disgruntled bear shifter agreed.

"Why don't you do something about it, Ian? You're skilled. You have decades of leadership under your belt," Dani suggested.

"I'm skilled at military command, sweetheart. What are you suggesting for me to do with it?"

"Well, I heard that Sheriff Vasco doesn't plan to run again. He's going to retire."

I stared at her. "Why didn't I think of that?" Russ had invited me to join the volunteer fire department weeks ago, and I'd told him I would consider it. Becoming Sheriff MacArthur would allow me to help even more people.

Dani grinned and lingered near Russ to tousle his hair. "Give it some serious thought at least. So how's Leigh? I thought she could use a friend and maybe I'd stop over to talk to her some."

I shook my head. "She's handling it all okay, but you'll have to wait. I sent her out to go shopping since the social worker plans to officially return Sophia to us today."

"You're letting her drive *your* vehicle?" Russ stared as if the shocking news was on par with letting her run free with my bank account.

"Yes. She's a grown woman. If I don't show she can be trusted, why should anyone else believe it?"

"Hey, darlin'? Would you go see where Trigger got off to?"

Dani arched one of her dark brows at Russ. She didn't fall for his excuse to get rid of her, but she humored him by walking away from the deck and into the grass, whistling a few times.

I knew the question was coming before it even left my pal's lips.

"Did you bond fully with her yet?"

"Not yet. Ever since my eagle recognized her I can't get her off my mind. The more I do for her, the deeper it pulls me in. I wanna tear the clothes off her most days, but she's in no shape to be feeling that kind of way."

Russ nodded. "It's like when she's hurtin', you're drowning in her pain, and her happiness is the only thing that can help you to breathe again."

"*Yes.*" I sagged into the seat and let out a frustrated groan.

"It's about time, old man. Revel in it and be happy you found her."

"Yeah. You're right. Maybe it's about time I told her what I am, too. I gotta let her know it isn't about wanting to get her on her feet anymore."

I needed to let her know we were soul mates.

LEIGH

Dad and I used to joke about Target being a middle-class Wal-Mart. Growing up the only child of a widower made me close to him, and in the final weeks of his life, I'd never felt more lonely. I should have realized it was time to cut Dennis loose from my life when he didn't try to help me through my grief, but if I had, I wouldn't have Sophia. She was my bright star and the one accident in my life I didn't regret.

I stared at the condoms on the shelf. We weren't using protection when we conceived Sophia, and I was sure we were both high when it happened anyway. Sex with Ian was inevitable in our near future. I knew we both wanted it, and it had to be safe between us.

I blindly grabbed a box and stuffed them beneath a box of diapers. After a few steps down the aisle, I considered my memory of Saturday morning. I scurried back to the display and swapped them for the larger size.

A stop at Redbox on the way home yielded a newly released horror movie from some big Hollywood studio with a monstrous special effects budget. After a few days of Ian's spy thrillers, I needed a break.

I wasn't the type to conduct frivolous shopping sprees. Ian had another plan and forbid me to return until I spent at least a grand. He claimed it would distract me until my 4 p.m. appointment with the social worker. With a trunk load of groceries and new clothes, I pulled into the drive an hour prior to the lady's expected arrival.

"Do you need help?" Ian called from the door.

"Yes, please."

We unpacked it all in record time. I'd run every kind of errand imaginable from visiting government offices to following up at the bank to finish paperwork for my new account.

The doorbell rang after I put the fresh crib sheet on Sophia's mattress. I beat Ian to the door and came face to face with the social worker charged with my case.

"Good afternoon, Mrs. MacArthur. Someone here is very thrilled to see you."

Eager to hold her again, I reached out and took my daughter from the caseworker. The woman entered after I stepped back to make room. I struggled to maintain my emotions and failed, tears sliding freely down my face no matter how I tried to keep them in.

"Thank you."

"You don't need to thank me, Mrs. MacArthur. You fulfilled the court's obligations."

At some point, I'd ceased to exist as merely 'Leigh' and had become the responsible and respectable Mrs. MacArthur.

"Is there something for me to sign?" I asked.

"No," she assured me. "You'll find everything has been handled regarding this matter. Enjoy your life with Sophia. I'm proud of you for coming so far."

"Thank you," I whispered again. I touched my cheek to the top of Sophia's curls and closed my eyes before sinking to the couch. We lay on the sofa and snuggled until Sophia's belly made her kick and squirm with hunger. The rest of my evening with her passed like a dream. She ate and received a bath before I dressed her in a pink onesie I'd washed the previous day. After a few soft coos and a cherubic smile, my baby fell asleep without a fuss.

I could have stood beside her crib watching her sleep for hours, but I rewarded myself for a job well done by unwinding with a cup of yogurt and a movie. Ian settled beside me as I pressed play. My dog lifted her head to look at Ian then collapsed into her bed again, too tired to approach for ear scratches. She had settled by my feet between the couch and Daddy's old coffee table. Ian leaned down to rub her.

"Where have you been all evening?" I asked.

"I thought I'd give you some space to be with Sophia. How's she liking it here so far?"

"She's a baby, silly. She'll like anywhere as long as she's dry, warm, and has a full tummy."

Ian chuckled. "Then maybe I should ask how her mama likes it here."

"Her mama loves it here," I replied. I pressed a few buttons and skipped to the main feature. Ian didn't budge from beside me. "I thought you hated horror movies."

"I like them from time to time." In other words, he didn't want to make me sit downstairs alone.

"You don't *have* to babysit me every night, Ian. I'm fine. I can watch a movie on my own."

Hurt flashed in his eyes. *Crap.* I swore internally at myself a few times for my poorly worded dismissal. "Ian, I'm sorry. I mean you don't have to feel responsible for entertaining me every night on top of everything else you've done."

"It's fine," he assured me. "I'm not your chaperone." The man rose from his seat despite my clumsy protests and apologies. He took his unfinished beer with him.

"Honestly, Ian, you're welcome to stay. You don't have to leave on my account."

His crooked, half-hearted smile didn't assuage my guilt. If anything, I was even more of a jerk for chasing him out of his own living room. "I have to leave early in the morning for work related stuff anyway. I really should get to sleep."

Long after he left, I still felt like an ungrateful bitch for chasing him off. Ian was a good man who deserved a lot better than what I gave him in return. I watched the rest of the movie without receiving any actual satisfaction then took a hot shower to ease my nerves. I soaked beneath the steady spray for longer than necessary then retired to my bedroom. Restless, I spent the next hours tossing and turning in bed.

No matter how long I tried, my conscience wouldn't allow me to sleep. I didn't want him to go away on one of his trips before I had the chance to apologize again.

There was no telling if he'd come back at all. With his dangerous career, anything could happen and I'd receive a knock on our door one day to see a uniformed soldier on the porch. He'd share his bad news, telling me my new husband wouldn't be coming home. Then I'd be a widow who regretted the last thing I said to my best friend was that he didn't need to babysit me.

Without another thought, I slipped from my bed and hurried across the hall into his room. He slept with his door open, the lights off, and the parted curtains allowed pale silver moonlight to shine over the large bed. His chest rose and fell with the even breathing rhythm of a deep sleep, so peaceful in his expression I hated to wake him at all.

"Ian?" I whispered in the dark as I laid my fingers over his bare arm. He was a slim man, but his build and preferred style of clothing painted a deceptive picture, concealing the muscles beneath.

The ground flew out from beneath me as I tumbled through the air. I hit the mattress beside him with the wind knocked from my lungs, his thick bicep across my neck. I couldn't even squeak, let alone scream. My hair fanned across his second pillow as the cool, untouched side of the bed cradled me. Somewhere in the back of my mind, beneath the absolute terror of course, I realized he had the softest mattress I'd ever felt.

"Leigh?" The pressure eased from my throat then rose completely away. "What the hell, woman? Are you all right? Did I hurt you?"

"No. You gave my heart a workout, but I'll survive it. I think." I hoped. I knew for damn sure the stiff object against my hip wasn't a gun.

"What's wrong? Why are you here at—" he glanced at the digital readout from the alarm on his bedside table "—almost midnight."

"I couldn't sleep, and I knew if I didn't come talk to you now, I might not have the chance until your business is settled and you come home and... that could be days from now." He'd warned me sometimes his contracts could take him away for a couple weeks at a time.

"I'll be back by Thursday. It's not a long trip. Mostly, I need to ask a favor from Argus, and if I don't spend the evening in San Antonio, he takes it as an insult."

He hadn't moved. Neither had the unyielding presence beneath the blanket. Only his sheets and a light comforter separated our bodies, my nightshirt shifted to an embarrassing level above my waist. He could see everything, from my chunky thighs to my plain white and blue striped cotton hipsters. At least they were brand new.

"Ian?"

Despite the darkness, I saw the way his eyes roved over me, slowly digesting my current state of undress. One of his hands gently tugged my nightshirt back into place.

"Didn't mean to scare you so bad, Leigh."

"It's okay," I whispered back. I waited for him to say something, but he never did.

His mouth crashed against mine in a sudden kiss, the lack of warning offering me no time to prepare. It took several pulse-pounding seconds until my brain caught up with my body and realized my sexy as sin phony husband was kissing *me*.

I moaned beneath his mouth and twisted to face his body completely. With a couple kicks, I managed to dislodge the blankets from beneath me until they were at the foot of the bed, confirming my suspicions. Every hard, muscled inch was exposed to my questing fingertips.

Our mouths broke apart, each of us dragging in a gulping lungful of air, but Ian didn't stop there. The scoop neckline of my shirt gave him free access to my throat. He nipped my collarbone and ran his hand over my thigh, raising goose bumps on my skin. "Are you on the pill, Leigh, because I don't have any—"

"I bought some. There's a package in my top dresser drawer."

"You bought condoms?"

"For us." His cock twitched against my hip. Apparently I'd given him the right answer, but as far as I was concerned, it was the only one.

He kissed the pounding pulse point at my throat before descending lower, reaching my left breast. His lips sealed around my nipple for a teasing suckle through the soft jersey cotton while I moaned and writhed beneath him.

"Wait for me," he whispered against my tit.

Bare as the day he was born, Ian left me behind and slipped from the room. I had the tantalizing view of his deliciously muscled naked ass, at least before he was out of sight.

While he was gone, I laid there fretting in bed, wondering what he thought of me. Each precious second played against my insecurities until he reappeared in the doorway less than a minute later. To say his absence had dulled the mood would be a lie — it worsened my anticipation. His hard cock bounced with his movements, swaying as he came to a stop beside me on the bed. Foil tore then I watched him glide the latex ring over his dick and wished I'd done it for him.

"Ian?" I murmured shyly as he lowered one knee to the bed and leaned over me. Our lips touched in another electrifying kiss.

"Shh."

My nightshirt rose a little higher until I had no choice but to raise my arms and allow him to remove it.

I wore no bra beneath the cute pink and white shirt, but I trusted in the darkness to hide my imperfections and round belly from his eyes. Silver stretch marks became the most prominent across my wide hips, something I wanted to conceal from him.

Ian eased back to kneel between my legs. He clicked the light on.

"Ian?"

"I want to see you."

A euphoric tingle of pure pleasure spread across my body from head to toe until fire seemed to consume every fiber of my being. I'd never felt particularly unattractive, but motherhood had added inches to my frame. Aside from my doctor, no man had seen me unclothed since the beginning of my third trimester, before the worst of the changes transformed my body. Ian was the first to see me this way. I wanted him to be the last.

His attentive eyes infused a sense of unfamiliar vulnerability, urging a hot flush to warm my cheeks. When I blushed, my entire upper body seemed to glow with color. He peeled my panties off last, and then there was nothing else to hide.

"You're breathtaking."

"Don't lie."

"I've never told an unnecessary lie in all my life, and I wouldn't now. You're beautiful, Leigh, and I love everything about the way you look. Every inch."

He bent above my body like a worshipper attending prayer at an altar. His lips skimmed my right hip and then my left while his thumb parted my folds. A little nibble to my thigh caught me off guard as much as the pressure circling my clit. He was an expert with his hands, merciless as he teased, using his fingers and mouth. Both of my nipples had hardened to unbearably tender peaks by the time his ascending path rose from my hip to my breast.

Moaning out his name was the proper encouragement. He filled me with one finger and then a second, pumping both digits in and out of my pussy. Eight long months had passed since the last time I had sex with Sophia's father, making me starved for the intimacy promised by Ian's touch.

"Ian. Ian, please."

"I don't think you're ready for me yet." A teasing tone filled his voice, accompanied by a husky hint of laughter. I twisted beneath him and raised my hips to the rhythm he set while plunging both digits in and out of me. If I wasn't ready now, I never would be. His fingers glistened on each stroke backward.

"Ian, if you don't fuck me right now, you're going to need those special operative skills to fight me off."

"You're adorable when you threaten me." Whether intimidated or not, he acquiesced to my demands, trading his fingers for his latex sheathed dick.

I'd always been afraid sex would never be the same

again, but Ian proved me wrong from the moment he began sliding into my pussy. Even soaking wet and ready for him, he was a tight fit my body struggled to accommodate. I stretched around his unyielding width and pleaded for more.

"God, you feel so sweet, Leigh," Ian breathed out. He wore an expression of immense concentration on his face.

His rhythm was slow and sensual, testing the way our bodies fit together. My nipples rubbed against his sculpted chest, tickled by the few black hairs scattered over his pecs. Over and over again, he brought our bodies together, taking me as his wife in body as well as in name. Within moments, he lost the careful composure and snapped his hips forward to bury into me full tilt. Bliss consumed me, curling my toes and making me cry out his name in a jubilant shout.

"Oh, baby. We haven't even started yet. You'll have a lot more to scream about in a minute," he promised.

I shivered beneath him in delight. My pussy clenched around his girth, a reflex brought by the sexy whisper. Ian chuckled and kissed my ear.

Ian shifted to stretch his body over mine, finding the perfect angle. With his hard muscles pillowed against my softness, I ran my fingers up and down his back and felt the way his back flexed beneath my fingers each time his body rolled forward.

With my legs around his waist, I yanked Ian in

closer and rolled him beneath me. The struggle slid him from my body, but a thrust of my hips reseated Ian's cock and reintroduced us to ecstasy. Before he could try to get the upper hand again, I leaned forward to brace my weight against his shoulders and undulated my hips until he swore and his eyes rolled back in his head. I wanted to lay my own claim.

"Don't stop, baby. Fuck, Leigh, don't stop." My breasts weren't more than a handful to fill his palms, but he squeezed and kneaded them eagerly, pinching the sensitive tips between his fingers. I clenched around his girth when he sat forward to capture one between his lips.

The partial loss of his dick introduced him to my g-spot. My muscles tensed and trembled on the verge of orgasm then I slammed him home again.

"I'm close, so close, Ian."

The base of his pelvis pressed flush against my clit in an intentional grind that pushed me over the edge. My climax was a series of starburst explosions, white bliss consuming every inch of my body. I spasmed atop him and threw my head back in a soundless cry.

He pulled me down by a handful of my hair. Something about the urgency in his kiss turned me on even more. For the first time in my life, I came a second time during sex, making my legs tremble and my body lay limp against his chest.

Post-orgasm contractions rippled along his cock

like aftershocks. My husband moaned against my cheek and stiffened in release.

Overwhelmed with pleasure, I barely registered he was moving me or turning off the light. He tossed the condom into the wastebasket then tugged me close. Sleep claimed Ian before I finished pulling the blanket over our bodies.

9

IAN

*L*eigh smelled the way I imagined an angel would smell; light and sweet with lavender undertones teasing across my senses when I awakened with her tucked beside me. After a moment of admiring her peaceful features while she slept, I disentangled from her body and crawled from the bed.

Fuck, I hated leaving her after our first night in bed. Disgruntled with my own plans, I showered and returned to my bedroom to dress. Indecision had me torn between making enough noise to awaken her on accident or intentionally rousing her for a goodbye kiss. I did neither. I clothed myself as silently as a ghost and jotted down a message on the notepad beside the bed.

Leigh,

My cell phone is the ideal way to reach me when I am away, but if technology lets us down, you're welcome to call my associate in San Antonio. It's the best way to get me if you require my immediate response for any emergency matters.

I taped a business card to the corner of the note. The matte rectangle announced the name and contact information of Argus Prescott, the alpha of San Antonio's wolf pack. He led an extravagant lifestyle afforded by old money and inherited wealth. Thanks to traffic, I arrived a little before noon.

The pack lived in the middle of nowhere far beyond the city limits in a massive, southern plantation style home. I pulled off the highway and punched a code into the security panel by the gate. Automated, heavy wrought iron gates swung open to allow me access onto a half-mile long drive. A dozen wolves — all omegas and low in the pack hierarchy — roamed freely on the grounds. Two of their gray faces watched my arrival from the bushes as I parked.

"Ian?" a feminine voice called.

My attention snapped to the opening door. It framed the youngest Prescott, Ceres, a sweet girl I'd once held on my lap as a child. She popped out onto the porch barefoot, clothed in only cutoff jeans and a sleeveless pink tank.

"Hey, sweetheart!" I greeted her.

With an excited squeal, she raced toward me across the drive. I caught my goddaughter mid-leap and swung her around in a circle while she giggled. Too much time had passed between my visits, and thanks to the obligations of my job, I'd missed out on her graduation from veterinary school.

"Uncle Ian! Why didn't you tell us you were coming?"

"Last minute plans," I told her. "I also came to the profound conclusion that I don't visit you guys enough these days now I'm back in the states for a while."

"You really don't. Come on. There's someone I want you to meet," she announced with a big smile on her face.

Her longtime friend and admirer, Thomas, met us at the door. Even though they were both just a couple years shy of thirty, I still referred to them as kids. I'd known him since he was a chunky nerd tagging along with her for ice cream during my visits. Shit, he was more ripped than me these days. Evidently, life as a werewolf agreed with him.

"Uh, Ceres, sweetheart. I know Thomas."

"But," she said while clinging to young man's brawny arm, "you don't know him as..." She raised one hand and flashed me the tattooed green and purple band around her left ring finger. Interlaced vines and tiny flowers decorated her skin. Thomas wore one in black without the flowers.

"When did that happen?"

"The tattoo or the proposal?" Thomas grinned at me.

"Both. Hell, last I knew, you were still playing hard to get while he ran in circles." A little more than a year ago, I'd chided her about making a decision. It wasn't right to lead a man on or to play games until he changed.

"I took her a week ago for the tattoo, but I asked over the summer. Now they're driving me crazy with wedding plans," Thomas explained.

"Don't envy you, man." I dodged a bullet by marrying Leigh in front of a magistrate in a courthouse.

"The wedding is this spring, and I want you to be there," Ceres said.

"Of course I'll be there."

"Tommy, would you let Dad know Uncle Ian is here?"

"Sure."

As he loped out of sight to inform the head of the house about my arrival, Ceres turned to me and punched me sharply in the shoulder.

"Fuck! What'd you do that for?"

She took my left hand and gestured to the plain

titanium band. "Why wasn't I invited? Was it a private ceremony? Who is she... or he?" Her green eyes grew a little wider, as if all of the pieces had finally fallen together. "Oh, my God, who is he, Uncle Ian? When do I get to meet him? Did you finally get married since it's legal now?"

"I'm not gay."

"Oh... awkward." She pressed her bare toes against the marble floor and cleared her throat. "Well, you never dated anyone that we've seen. Sorry," she babbled out.

"So you thought I was gay?" Torn between horror and laughter, I settled on a grin. "There's nothing wrong with being gay, but I'm sorry to disappoint you, sweetie. I'm straight."

"So who is she? What's her name?"

"Her name is Leigh."

Ceres perked up a little. She leaned in close again, all in my space, and sniffed my shirt in a way reminiscent of a dog. I used to think it was cute when she'd do it as a child, and it hadn't changed. "Human? I smell her on your clothes. She smells like cookies. Oh, come on, Uncle Ian. This isn't one of your cases in Saudi Arabia or whatever, can't you tell me something?"

I sighed. "I knew you'd give me the fifth degree, and I'm absolutely prepared to answer a thousand questions once I've talked to your dad."

"And rehearsed your story," she said. Argus stepped into view with Thomas alongside him. "Hi, Daddy."

His arrival saved me from a full-blown interrogation.

"Ian," Argus greeted me with warmth. "You don't normally visit in person unless you need something important, old friend. What's the problem this time?"

"Argus, you wound me. Didn't we help you when those hunters were calling for open season on wolves?"

"You did, and we're grateful for it, which is why I'm not plucking your feathers and throwing you out my door. You came in the middle of a busy time for us."

I grinned. Every time was a busy time for the wolves who had their fingers in more environmental protection ventures than I could count. Argus was a banker by career — my personal banker *and* lawyer. Whenever I needed something, I usually phoned in requests or sent them by fax. For the big stuff beyond his profession, I visited him in person.

"I need some of your wolves to do a sweep in the woods. Just some tracking work, nothing too big. If you think they'll spare someone, I'll need a raven or two for aerial surveillance. I'll need them for about a week, and I'll pay all of them well for their time."

Ravens and wolves worked closely together. Their symbiotic alliance meant one was never far from the other. Where a wolf pack existed, ravens usually made their roost in a nearby town.

"Whoa, whoa, whoa. Hold it. Ravens too? What the hell's happening?"

We went into Argus' personal office and discussed everything. I held no details back from my friend and painted a perfect picture of the drug problem creeping into Quickdraw. He listened and took notes, occasionally interrupting me to ask another question.

"Do you believe the town police are involved?"

"Not all of them. At least a few are on the up and up, but I'm concerned about the police chief's tendency to sweep things under the rug. I don't trust him."

"We'd better get Thomas in here then since he leads the second pack. We'll need a couple of his wolves."

"Thomas?"

"Yes. We've grown enough recently to require dividing our numbers." Argus dropped his gaze to the titanium ring on my finger. "Why didn't you bring your new wife with you?"

I imagined a dozen wolves greeting her with doggy kisses and wagging tails. Smirking, I suppressed the urge to laugh out loud at the ridiculous imagery filling my head. "She doesn't exactly know about all of this yet."

"Good luck. We recently brought a human into the fold, so I understand the challenge."

Once he called Thomas into the room, the three of us drew out our battle plans for Quickdraw. The younger alpha made arrangements with two of his friends from the raven clan to keep their schedules open in the coming weeks then promised his own help when needed.

Later, a chat over drinks allowed all of us to catch up on each other's lives.

Argus was newly single after thirty years of marriage, but he looked forward to the upcoming wedding of his only child. Eager as ever to share with me, Ceres revealed more about the upcoming wedding.

"You're really going to love our fiancée, Emma. She's a sweetheart. You guys can tell each other stories from your tribes!"

"Huh? What do you mean there's a second bride?" My eyes bugged out despite my effort to keep a straight face.

"Because Tommy was born human, we have a third fated mate," Ceres explained. "And maybe if you would bring your ass here to see us more often, you'll get to meet her."

Unlike other shifters, werewolves had the unusual ability to transform normal people during the full moon. As a former human, Thomas had what we called a split soul. His human half and feral half would always be at constant war. "So which one of you goes on the books?"

Ceres raised her hand and grinned. "I'll be the legal wife. We plan to visit the courthouse a couple days prior then do the big ceremony here at Dad's place with the three of us."

"I don't know whether to call you a lucky bastard or to feel pity for you," I said to Thomas. Multiple life mates could be a typical part of life for some shifters, especially those who participated in pack or herd life. Lioness shifters like my friend Sasha were often four or five women to a single exhausted, overworked man.

"I value my life, so I'll say lucky," Thomas replied. "They like to talk a lot, and I wouldn't survive the night if I said otherwise."

Ceres shot him a dirty look. "Okay, enough about us, Uncle Ian. What about you? How'd you meet her? What's she like? Do you have a photo of her? Is she on Facebook? Oh, my God, can I go friend her?" Ceres fired one question after the next.

"Here. She doesn't do social media, but I have this photo of her and the kid." I passed my cell phone to her. I'd snapped the photo of Leigh and Sophia's reunion when the social worker brought her by.

"She's so cute!" Ceres squealed over Sophia's picture. "And I love Leigh's hair. Oh, please, you have to bring her out for a visit. She, Emma, and I would have so much fun."

"Soon, sweetie, I promise. I have to take care of some things first." I caught them up on the recent business with Leigh only recently regaining full custody of her child.

"You married her because she kicked her drug problem and needed help?" Thomas clarified, raising his brows.

"I think it's sweet," Ceres said before elbowing him. "Don't listen to Tommy. Bring her back next time so all of us can meet her, Uncle Ian. Please? I promise we'll tell the omegas to keep out of sight, and we'll all do our best to pretend to be human. I mean, unless you do choose to tell her."

"I've given it some serious consideration. She's smart, and she'll begin noticing things eventually. I can't risk her finding out some other way, like the incident with Russ and Dani."

Argus winced. "Yeah. Sounds like you're making the right choice."

After dinner, the kids split and went back to their own home. I hung around with Argus for a while longer then eventually retired to the guest room where I dropped onto the edge of the bed. My silent cell phone taunted me. Not a single call from Leigh. I bit the bullet and phoned her instead.

What am I doing? She's not a child. She can fend for herself now, and she's more than proven she isn't the same drug-dependent woman. She doesn't need me checking in on her.

But I wanted to hear her voice. The call wasn't to check up on her — it was purely for me. I dialed my house line and waited with my breath held until she picked up the phone on the third ring.

"MacArthur residence." She sounded out of breath, winded like she'd sprinted for the line.

"Hi, Leigh. Are you okay?"

"Was exercising. One sec."

"Why are you exercising?"

There was a pause on her end of the line, then a quiet, nervous laugh. "I just felt like exercising."

Is she doing it for me? A cocky little voice whispered in my mind, bringing a smug smile to my face. "I think you're perfect just the way you are."

Leigh didn't answer right away. I pictured her with a rosy flush on her face. "Anyway, I hope you didn't call earlier and I missed it. Daniela invited me over for dinner."

"Why don't you go and buy a cell phone," I encouraged her.

"I didn't want to waste money. You were so generous and the amount you gave me was enough to cover the household needs. It just seemed stupid to get a cell phone, too."

"It's not a waste. You have Sophia with you and

you'll be driving places for Gram and yourself. We'll have a line added to my plan."

"I don't know, Ian—"

"I insist. It's a smart purchase. How's Sophia by the way?"

"She's great. Your grandmother complained about you leaving again. She thinks since you've retired you shouldn't be doing these jobs anymore."

"Don't listen to her, especially since this job has nothing to do with the government or our military. I'm visiting a friend to discuss some important business negotiations, and they sort of sweet-talked me into bringing you along next time," I said.

"Really?"

"Really. My goddaughter, Ceres, is planning to be married in the spring, so we're both invited. Fair warning: she's incredibly excited about meeting you and thought I was gay until now."

A moment of stunned silence was followed by the cutest peal of giggles I'd ever heard.

"You definitely aren't gay," Leigh said. I pictured her blushing red and heard it in her voice. When I got home, we'd have to talk about the night we shared together and which direction it would take our blossoming relationship. It was imperative for her to understand it wasn't a one-night thing, unless of course, she wanted it to be.

I hoped she didn't want that to be the end of it.

"Anyway, I'm leaving sometime in the morning and should be home by lunch time unless I hit some serious traffic on I-45."

"I'll have lunch waiting for you."

I wished her a good night and ended the call after she bid me to have the same. As I settled down for bed, my confession to Leigh remained on my mind. It couldn't wait another day.

*J*an returned around noon from his trip to San Antonio as I was completing a few household chores. Petunia barked loudly to announce his SUV pulling into the driveway.

"Wow. It looks great in here. You were busy while I was gone."

"I wanted it to be spotless when you came home. I even cleaned the fan blades. You're just on time, too. The pizza delivery man left right before you pulled in."

He opened the box and whistled. "Sausage and mushroom. You ordered my favorite. Wanna eat on the deck?"

"Yes!" I shouted it a little too enthusiastically. His curious glance and raised brows brought heat to my cheeks.

"You look great when you blush."

Emboldened by the affection in Ian's sunlight-colored eyes, I stepped forward to touch his face, tracing my index finger down his jaw and over the soft scruff he never seemed to shave. He had traces of silver in his beard I hadn't noticed before. It suited him, adding a hint of contrasting maturity to his striking features.

Turning his head, he brushed his lips against my fingers. My belly clenched as if he'd kissed me between my thighs. "We should eat before the food gets cold."

"Or before Sophia wakes up," I added.

Ian moved the pizza and breadsticks while I carried the lemonade pitcher and our glasses. We settled on the deck with the baby monitor close at hand and enjoyed the cool autumn breeze snaking in between the trees to dishevel my bangs. The sweet scent of earth and woods surrounded us, blended with fragrant pizza sauce and garlic bread sticks.

We chowed down and shared friendly conversation about his day with his old friend and my evening out with the neighbors. I didn't do long distance drives well and always fell asleep, so I admired his ability to make the five hour trek in high spirits. I couldn't wait to return with him.

"Leigh?"

"Hmm?" I had so much food in me, the only thing able to improve my day would be a nap stretched out in Ian's massive feather-soft bed.

Ian's expression changed, taking on a worried appearance. His brows creased, alerting me to something heavy on his mind. Our short friendship and even shorter marriage didn't hamper my ability to read him like an open book.

"What is it?"

"I decided to run for sheriff in the next election." The apprehensive expression remained.

"Won't you have to be here a lot if you run for sheriff, Ian? I thought you liked going away with your squad and taking up your government contracts."

"I do," he said. "And I can still do that, it just won't be as often as it used to be." I wanted to leave my seat to rub his tense shoulders. "But I want to do something for this area besides throwing my money around at people. Sophia deserves to grow up somewhere safe. To be honest, when I married you, I knew then I'd be cutting back on the work I do."

"This is great news!" I leaned out of my seat to throw my arms around his neck and kiss his cheek. "People around here respect you. You'd make a great sheriff."

"That's not everything. We need to discuss one more thing first. There's something I want to show you... and I know it's going to seem crazy, but I need you to have an open mind." He returned my embrace then ran his fingers through my hair, smoothing strands back from my face.

I raised my brows. His pale, champagne colored eyes watched me closely. "Okay? Ian, you're driving me crazy with this somber mood. Just tell me everything."

"The thing I need to show you has an incredible amount of importance for me, Leigh. I need to know I can trust you to keep this to yourself, because it affects more than me."

Was he going to let me in on something related to one of his top-secret government jobs? My pulse sped and my mouth went dry, prompting me to pour another glass of lavender lemonade from the pitcher. I sipped it nervously and cleared my throat before answering him. "Ian, I'll keep any secret you want me to keep. What's wrong?"

"I think it'll be easier if I show you first. Then we can talk about it."

Ian rose from his seat and pulled off his shirt, in the sexy way where guys grabbed a t-shirt by the back of the collar.

"Are you giving me a strip tease? You didn't get a tramp stamp of my name or something while away, did you?" I tried to ease the tension with some humor, sensing he needed it as much as I did.

Ian chuckled nervously and unfastened his jeans. I sat up straighter in the chair and stared at him. My child napped indoors, tucked safe and sound in her crib with a monitor on the table beside it, so if Ian was fishing for sex, he'd picked an excellent time for a second intimate encounter.

"Ian?"

His pants dropped and his boxers followed. He was perfect from head to toe, the very idea of masculinity. Because hard muscle and a lean build made his age indeterminable, I wouldn't have guessed my husband to be a day over thirty-five, despite the generous amount of silver in his dark hair. Ian's youthful features contradicted the loss of his chestnut brown coloring.

I lost the battle against my willpower and let my eyes drop below his waist. Even in its unaroused state, his cock was nearly as large as some of the guys I'd dated in the past when erect.

"Just remember it's me. Don't freak."

"Ian, I'm not going to freak because a hot naked man is standing in front of me. I'm freaking because you're being mysterious. What are you—?"

Ian's slim body contorted and a loud, cracking sound filled the air. A tiny shriek ripped from my throat. Before my eyes, he jerked one direction and shrank as a rush of ivory and brown plumage materialized into being. It may have all happened in a split second, but for me, it lasted an eternity. Ian wasn't there anymore; in his place, a proud American bald eagle stood on the wood patio deck. The eagle I touched in my very own yard less than six weeks ago.

When the raptor came closer to me, I slammed against the bricks beside the patio door. At some point, I must have leapt from my seat and stumbled against the back of the house.

It's Ian. I tried to tell myself it was Ian. The bird hadn't spirited him away, and he hadn't pulled a disappearing act worthy of Houdini. The bird *was* him. I leaned against the house until the threat of fainting was long over. My bird was him.

My heart leapt into my throat. Speaking became difficult, like a fist clenched my neck.

"Ian?" I whispered.

The bird tilted his head. They had the same gorgeous eyes, a too pale shade reminiscent of rose gold. How had I never drawn the comparison until now?

My racing pulse demanded for me to run, but the sensible part of me saw the man beneath the feathers and knew he'd never hurt me. Fighting against instinct, I crouched low and raised one trembling hand to the top of the eagle's head. I stroked him then let my fingers travel lower until I petted the silky feathers covering his breast.

"You're so... so gorgeous. I don't understand." I felt dizzy again. "I need to sit down. I need to sit down."

Ian was Ian again, a man crouching with me, his strong hands on my shoulders steadying me. Speechless, I couldn't even make lame come-ons or joke about his nudity.

"I'm a shapeshifter, Leigh.

"Not possible. *This* isn't possible." It became a struggle to control my breathing, and I was in danger of hyperventilating. Quick intakes of air whistled in and out of my lungs. "I am dreaming. Any minute I am going to wake up because you're walking through the front door and I've been asleep on the couch taking a nap."

"I knew from the moment I first saw you, that you were the woman I wanted. Because I'm a shifter and because I've been drawn to you. You met me once like this Leigh, because I wanted to see you again after I took you home."

The light-headed feeling didn't abate. When I wobbled again, Ian coaxed me to sit on the deck. I'd recently swept it clean of leaves and debris at least. "Like love at first sight?" It was hard having a conversation with a naked person, harder when the naked person had transformed from the shape of a bird.

"Sort of. You could call it such, I guess. I could have resisted if I wanted to, but the thing is, Leigh, I didn't. When I saw the way the people at church treated you, I couldn't let it pass."

"So you helped me because of what?"

"Because no one deserves to be treated that way, Leigh. Hell, I'd have stepped in for anyone, but finding you at the same time..." He sighed. "Come on. Let's get you off the ground."

Ian helped me up to my feet, but I stumbled against him and into his hard body. His strong arms surrounded me without hesitation.

"What's this mean, Ian? For me and Sophia. For... us."

"It means I don't only want you for a year, or until you're out of school and on your feet, Leigh. I want you for the rest of my life, for as long as you'll have me. I never intended to let you go without a fight. When I married you, I hoped you'd eventually come to want me, too."

And then I had visited his room in the middle of the night. I trembled, distracted by the memory of his lips against mine. I wanted to be afraid. I wanted to be terrified of a man who could turn into a wild animal in the span of a second, but in my heart, I knew he was the same Ian who rescued me from my shitty life decisions. Cold from the shock, I pressed closer against him to reap the benefits of his body heat.

"Are you okay, Leigh?"

"I'm fine," I whispered.

"If you want out, I'll understand."

"I didn't say that." The idea of ending it all and walking way away seemed scarier than the secret he'd revealed. I'd have to be a fool to go.

Sophia's sudden, piercing shriek interrupted our

conversation. "I have to check her... um..."

"We'll finish this when you're done," Ian assured me.

I returned inside, glancing once over my shoulder to see him gathering his clothes off the deck. By the time I'd finished comforting my infant by changing a wet diaper, Ian had brought in our leftover goodies and clothed himself in his jeans. That was regrettable. We crossed paths as he exited the kitchen and moved our conversation to the living room where we settled on opposite ends of the same couch.

When Ian didn't speak first, I bit the bullet and started us off. "So... You turn into an eagle. Bet that was useful in the Air Force."

Ian's faint smile held a trace of amusement. "It was, actually. I'm the leader of a special group of individuals, each of us with a unique skill set related to our shifter traits."

"Wait a minute. Wasn't Russell in your squad? Are Dani and Russ eagles too?"

His rich, deep laughter filled the room. "No. Not eagles, sweetie. Dani is as human as you are, Leigh. My kind are incredibly rare."

Ian gave me a lot to think about and too many questions to ask at once. If Russ wasn't a human or an eagle, what was he? And had Ian settled for me due to the lack of women among his own species?

"I can see the question in your eyes. Russ is a bear."

Shit. A bear of a man and an actual bear.

"Does Dani know?" I whispered.

"Yeah, she does. Took Russ a while to tell her, though, and I didn't want to make the same mistake with you, Leigh. I wanted to tell you as soon as I knew I could trust you."

"I want to be pissed at you. I want to be so mad that you kept it from me. But another part of me wants to kiss you, because I missed you so much."

"I'll take the kisses," he offered helpfully.

So would I. We closed the distance between us at the same time, practically leaping at one another across the couch. His fingers tangled in my hair and our lips came together in a hard, bruising press. We were frenzied, as if a day apart had starved us of each other.

Ian tore away my camisole without a word. Warm sunlight spilled through the window over my bared breasts and upper body. He didn't need a bedside lamp to see me, and I didn't give a damn that he could. His mouth lowered to one nipple and then the other, delivering playful nips to the tip of each breast until they were stiffly budded peaks.

Without thinking, I snuck one hand in the waist of my pajama bottoms. I was soaked, and having Ian so close brought out the shameless side of me I never knew existed before. I circled my clit until his fingers closed around my wrist.

"You're not allowed to touch yourself," Ian whispered. His lips were at my ear, delivering a teasing nibble against my unpierced lobe.

"No? Why not?"

"Because it's *my* duty to give you pleasure, Leigh. I'm your husband."

A shiver coursed through me as Ian knelt and pulled down my capris. He tugged aside my bikini style panties before tonguing my slit. He lapped at my folds, making my body tense and my heart race with every parting lick and the discovery of my clit. Within seconds, he proved he was as skilled with his tongue as he was with his hands, introducing me to ecstasy I'd never experienced before. His lips closed around my clit, trapping the tiny nerve bundle for a series of torturous strokes. Just when I was on the verge of climax, he stopped and kissed the crease of my thigh instead.

The tiniest twitch of my hands toward my body resulted in his longer fingers encircling my wrists. He pinned me down with the lightest touch. It was all he needed.

"I couldn't wait to get back to you to do this, Leigh."

"Ian, don't stop... I need... I need..." I needed him inside me. To feel our bodies connected together as one.

"I know what you need." The sexy confidence in his voice convinced me it was true.

"Ian," I pleaded softly, squirming on my back until his mouth descended again. He lavished fleeting licks and split my folds with his tongue. At the end, he sealed his mouth around my clit and suckled.

Molten heat crashed over my body and swept me on the tide of passion. I arched my back and gripped his salt and pepper hair in one hand until the last contraction ended and I became a boneless heap on the couch. Afterward, Ian, traced lazy circles over my thigh. I moaned something unintelligible. My orgasm had made my limbs feel heavy as lead weights.

"Do you think I'm finished with you already, sweetheart?" His index finger teased between my thighs until my legs parted again and yielded access. One brush of his fingertip made me shudder again.

"Ian..." He bent his head and kissed me, brushing our lips tenderly at first. I could taste myself on his tongue, a discovery that turned me on more than anything. An overwhelming urge came over me to have Ian in my mouth, to feel the hot pulse of his cum. Somehow, it reinvigorated me.

"Bedroom. We need the bedroom," I gasped, pulling away from him.

"It's just us, Leigh. In our house."

Ian fished a foil square from his discarded jeans and tore it open. Licking my lips in anticipation, I watched him roll it over his hard length. He was definitely well-endowed for a bird-man, and I wouldn't have him any other way.

"My eagle wants to bond with you and claim you, Leigh. There's no undoing it for me after this, baby. I need to know if you want this. If you truly want *this*."

"I want you exactly as you are."

Ian flipped me onto my belly and dragged my lower half off the couch onto my knees. Before I could speak another word, he nudged his dick between my folds and gradually penetrated me, drawing out our merging one tedious second after the next. A pitiful moan parted my lips.

"Leigh?" I heard the question in his tone: had he hurt me this time?

"Don't fucking stop," I growled at him.

My encouragement inspired a series of ruthless thrusts. He took me hard and fast from behind, slapping our bodies together, and his pelvis against my softer ass cheeks. Each slam jerked me forward into the couch. His arm was like a steel band around my waist, securing me against him while one hand palmed my breast.

It didn't matter that it was only our second lovemaking. We both knew how we liked it and what we wanted from each other. Once we found the rhythm, we kept an urgent and desperate pace. My every nerve was alive and humming with power. Without me having to ask or guide him, Ian's other hand dipped below my belly and traveled south until his fingers curved between my thighs. He touched my clit with confident fingers and introduced me to ecstasy.

"Close, so close," I panted out.

His lips skimmed my ear. "You're going to be more than close, baby."

I clenched around his dick. Fuck, I loved it when he called me baby.

In a torturous move, Ian slowed his pace until the imminent threat of my release dimmed. Then, just as swiftly, he pounded into me with renewed vigor. The back and forth pace drove me toward my finish.

The first orgasm was comparable to detonating a stick of dynamite, exploding and igniting the next charge in the set. Arching my back, I screamed as the next rolling series of endless contractions lit through my soul, calling his name over and over more times than I could count. Through it all, his motions never ceased.

Just when I thought it was over, Ian's backstroke set off another chain reaction as he stiffened behind me in climax. His breathless reaffirmation told me exactly what I needed to hear.

"*Mine.*"

When I came to, Ian's concerned face was gazing down at me. He sat cross-legged on the floor with me over his lap, a sweaty sheen still glistening over his shoulders.

"What happened?" The sound of my hoarse voice startled me. One moment I was experiencing the best climax of my life, and in the next, I was staring up at my lover from the floor.

"You passed out," he answered with a sheepish look on his face.

"I passed out during sex?"

"I think you were still kind of hanging on at the end there, so, technically, it was after sex, but yeah."

I tried to lift one hand to weakly swat at him, but it only fell back to my side again. "Is that a shifter thing?"

"It's actually rare, hon. Or so I've been told."

"Nngh... maybe it's a credit to your sexual prowess that it made *me* faint then."

Once I assured Ian I was fine, he helped me from the floor and stole a tender kiss. We spent most of the afternoon sprawled on the couch together while I listened to the sound of his strong heartbeat. He was right. It was our home and no one could see us enjoying it in the way we wanted. It wouldn't last once Sophia was older, but for now, I planned to enjoy every minute, especially until she awakened from her nap.

"I never meant to mislead you, Leigh," Ian broke the silence.

"I know." I raised my head to look into his eyes, and for once, I saw the vulnerability beneath his masculine bravado. Ian was tough, but he needed me as much as I needed him. "Your secret is safe with me. I promise."

*L*eigh forbade me to from telling Dani and Russ she was in the know, but I warned her Russ would be able to smell the change in her scent and know we had bonded.

"So? Bonding doesn't mean you told me the truth about his furry side," she pointed out. "Or your feathered one for that matter. Let me have a little fun with him."

"True."

Our friends visited us for lunch a couple days later. While they were around, we made Thanksgiving plans for a big dinner at my house to save my grandmother the obligation of attempting to cook. The women shuffled around the kitchen while Russ and I drank beers in front of the television and discussed plans for an upcoming trip to Israel.

"Food is ready. Here, give Sophia to me," Leigh said.

"Nah, I got her, babe," I said.

"How are you going to eat with her flailing her fists into your plate?" my wife demanded.

"I'll manage," I insisted. "It can't be worse than trying to eat with Russ nearby while on a surveillance mission in the east."

Leigh and Dani promptly burst into giggles. My squad mate's betrayed look only added to our amusement.

"You think he's a grump now when he's hungry? You haven't seen how scary he gets when he hasn't had a full meal in a couple days," I continued.

"Russ is such a teddy bear; I can't imagine him being scary at all," Leigh said.

Amidst her own giggles, Dani shot an affectionate look at Russ. She eased behind the couch and leaned over his shoulder to kiss his cheek. I didn't realize Leigh's pun was intentional until they continued during our lunchtime chatter.

"You ought to send Leigh over for firearms lessons, Ian."

"Bear with me a second, Russ. Shooting lessons? Like me firing a real gun?"

"Hell yeah, why not? Dani shoots as well as some of the men I've seen in the military. I'd suggest for this guy to teach you, but he's shit with a handgun anyway."

"I am not," I protested. "I just prefer a rifle."

"What do you think, Ian?" Leigh turned to face me.

"I think it's a good idea. Crime is sort of on the rise lately anyway, so it won't do any harm for you to learn."

"Hopefully, you can put a change to that once you get in office as sheriff," Dani said.

"I haven't won yet. The election isn't for months."

Both girls laughed as if my chance of losing the election was an impossibility. "Yeah, sure. You'll win by a landslide, Ian. This town loves you and what your family's done for it. Betty's already got a sign in her yard," Leigh said.

"Where the hell did she get a sign?" I asked.

"I kind of put it there yesterday when Sophia and I went to sit with her." Leigh grinned. "It was her idea. We went out to the sign maker in town and had a couple dozen made up. We could *barely* contain our excitement."

"Hey, Leigh, where did you get this?" Dani called from the kitchen.

Russ pulled me aside the moment Leigh left the room. They remained in the kitchen to ogle some of Leigh's recent shopping discoveries.

"What's with all the bear puns from her today, man? Am I paranoid and imagining it or does she know?"

"She knows," I confessed. "She wouldn't let me warn both of you."

"Asshole. That little brat had me sweating bullets." Russ playfully slugged me in the shoulder.

I grinned at him and took out my phone to check my messages. "They're here. Thomas and Ceres are going to park their truck at the community center. They brought two ravens."

"Aw shit. Are we going now?"

"Might as well get it done, don't you think?"

"I guess so. Dani's kind of grumpy with me anyway. Maybe an evening away will give her a chance to cool off."

"Really? She seemed fine to me."

"It comes and goes, man. Sometimes I wonder if all this shifter stuff is smothering her. Today she's fine, but last night was just damned awful. Everything I did upset her."

"Think a couple days away will help? Dani can have some space to relax if she's feeling overwhelmed. Maybe it's time to arrange for a weekend campout with Taylor and Juni soon," I suggested.

"You know how Sasha feels when we leave her out," Russ mentioned.

"Yeah, but..." I whistled. "Shit, I hate leaving her out, too, but she's still sore over splitting with Taylor. I didn't want to rub salt into a raw wound for either of them."

"They'll get over it. We'll only make it worse if we keep trying to handle them separately."

"You're right. I'm a little weirded out that you're being the sensible one, but you're right."

Russ slugged me in the arm. "Anyway, let's go get our lunch."

~

LEIGH

The bite of a chilly afternoon wind whipped against my cheeks. As soon as the men had declared they were heading into the woods in their shifter forms, Dani and I spilled onto the patio deck with them. Maybe it should have been weird to see Russ stripping down in front of me, or even weirder for Ian to do it with another woman present, but nothing about their behavior seemed sexual.

"This isn't awkward like I expected it to be," Dani whispered.

"It's for science," I replied.

We nodded.

"We'll be back for dinner," Ian assured me. My husband handed off his clothes, which I folded after giving him a chaste kiss to his cheek.

"Why are you taking off naked into the woods?" I asked.

"Need to know info, hon," Ian said.

"And I don't need to know."

"You got it."

"Fine, fine. You two be careful then. Don't, you know, get waylaid by some flirty lady eagle wanting to hatch chicks."

"Never any fear of that."

The transformations happened in a blink of an eye. One minute there were two smoking hot naked men on the porch, and the next second there were wild animals. Ian flapped his powerful wings and took to the air, showing off by soaring high then plummeting toward the ground like a feathered bullet. Even Russ in bear form seemed to roll his eyes.

Ian landed on the wooden patio railing and leaned close until I understood his silent request. I dipped down to smooch his beak; then a satisfied eagle flew away into the distance. After Russ trundled into the woods, we sighed and headed back into the kitchen.

"Movies with Sophia then?" I suggested.

With two mega-sized bowls of ice cream and a bag of popcorn to share between us, we settled in the living room with a romantic comedy. Sophia enjoyed tummy time on the floor at our feet, babbling at a plush patriotic designed eagle toy. She gummed on the soft beak and squished the blue wings in her chubby fists.

"I love your dress. Where did you get it?"

"I picked it up from the new thrift store in town.

What I like most is the skirt, because I can carry my revolver under it," Daniela explained. She hiked up the dress to mid-thigh level and revealed the holster. Her legs were a little slimmer than mine and I envied her.... her ample bust line.

"I don't think a thigh holster would fit me."

"Russ had this made for me after I passed the course for my concealed handgun license."

"I've never shot a gun in my li—"

Tires squealed in the dirt road in front of my house then the windows imploded, showering the carpet with glass shards. Projectiles sailed through the open space and thumped into the walls.

My terrified dog fled upstairs. As my instincts kicked in, I threw myself onto the floor and wriggled into place on top of Sophia to shield her. "Should we run?" I called up to Dani.

"No! Just stay down!" she urged me. On her hands and knees, she pushed with her body to shove the sofa on an angle between the windows and us. "Fuck, I can't text Russ. I have his phone!" She dialed 911 and put it on speakerphone.

"911. What is your emergency?" a relaxed voice spoke to us.

"Someone is shooting into our house!" I yelled back, fearing I couldn't be heard.

"Where is your location?"

I rattled off the address and hoped the operator

understood my shaking voice. She calmly repeated it back and let us know a car was on its way and to stay on the line.

"Can you make it into a safe place?"

"N-no, and I have my baby with me. Please hurry."

I didn't dare grab Sophia and run for it while bullets flew through the destroyed windows into our living room. More glass shattered behind my head, indicating Ian's television was trashed. With my body curled over my squalling, kicking child, I was her first line of defense against any wayward bullets. We had nowhere to run and no place we could hide, but in the midst of all the shooting, the door slammed open and heavy steps thudded through the entrance way.

An African-American man burst into the foyer with a scrawny white guy beside him. Both needed a good meal, and only one had his teeth. They leveled handguns into the living room as they spun to face us. "Get the fuck down and—"

Dani didn't give them the chance to finish his command. Her revolver barked loudly and the black guy fell thrashing to the ground. The toothless white guy remained upright beside him and fired a round at my friend. A bullet missed her head by a narrow margin, carrying forward into some knickknacks on Ian's fireplace mantle instead.

"Bitch, drop the fucking gun!" When Dani didn't lower her weapon, he pulled the trigger and shot her.

Dani jerked and stumbled back as a bullet slammed into her body. She squeezed off rounds until the revolver clicked dry and the other shooter went down.

"Dani!" I cried.

She stumbled to the couch and slumped in the corner, profuse amounts of dark blood staining her new dress. A steady trickle seeped from a bullet wound on her left shoulder. My fledgling knowledge of human anatomy told me it was close to a large blood vessel, but probably hadn't punctured it.

One of the shooters wasn't out. He sat up with a groan and swung his gun arm up. Without thinking, I rushed toward him, snatching the lamp from the table and yanking its cord from the wall. I bashed him over the head before he could aim then secured his fallen firearm. They weren't dead, but I didn't trust leaving a weapon within reach.

"My friend's been shot!" I screamed at the phone when I returned.

"Fuck, fuck, fuck!" someone shouted outside. A growl preceded several gunshots then a noise resembling a dog's whimper.

"Do something, dude!" another voice shouted.

"You didn't say the motherfuckah got attack dogs 'round here!" With the windows blasted out, their voices carried across the lawn into the room.

From where I knelt beside Dani, I couldn't see

much out the window but besides an ancient red Nissan parked by the road. A figure in a dark hoodie jumped into the bed of the truck then the driver peeled down the road.

"Are you and Sophia okay?" Dani asked.

"Forget us, we're fine!" I don't know what had come over me, but I went into action. Using a baby blanket for a makeshift cradle sling, I secured Sophia against me to provide her comfort. She continued to squall, but the angry red color faded from her cheeks. With her beginning to quiet, I doubled over and folded an afghan from the back of the couch and guided Dani onto the hard floor. "I'm going to apply pressure to this, okay, Dani? And to your back where it exited."

We remained that way until sirens heralded the arrival of EMS and the police. According to the paramedic who helped her onto the stretcher, my friend's injury wasn't a gusher, more of a slow trickle, which meant it hadn't hit a major artery. I'd probably saved her from going into shock.

"Let me grab my purse, and I'll come with—"

"No! Stay here to tell the boys what happened," Dani insisted. "They'll be home soon. You need to be here to tell them what happened."

"Are you sure you'll be okay?"

Dani smiled weakly at me as they wheeled her into the ambulance. "Positive. These vans carry morphine."

Once I had Sophia settled and in her crib, the cops

asked me question after question, having me repeat the story long after they seemed satisfied. They took photographs and waited for my husband to arrive while I nervously shot glances at the kitchen. I'd left Russ and Ian's clothing on the patio table outside.

"I don't *know* where my husband went."

"Does Mr. MacArthur have a cell phone number where you can reach him, Leigh?"

It was on the kitchen table. I sighed. "Ian went for a walk. I think he and our neighbor were planning to set up a deer stand or something somewhere, and he owns a couple hundred acres or so. There's no telling where they went."

"I'm right here. What the hell's going on here?" A glance over my shoulder revealed Ian striding from the kitchen. Russ wasn't far behind him.

"We heard the sirens. What's happening?" Russ stared into the living room then at the blood stains on the couch. His face went white as a sheet. "Where's Dani?"

"She told me to stay behind and tell you guys what happened." I relayed the story to them in detail like I had for the cops, and once I was done, Russ took off for the hospital in Ian's SUV.

"Are you sure you're all right?" Ian demanded. His eyes darted toward Sophia's bedroom door then swept over my body. His hands followed, quickly assessing whether or not I had sustained an injury. He lingered at the blood on my jeans.

"I'm fine. I'm fine, Ian. We're both fine!" I tried to convince him when he moved as if to dart to Sophia's room next. "Sophia's okay, too. Not a scratch on either of us. It's just... I was so afraid, and I didn't know what to do, but somehow I did everything right." The rest of my attempt to speak broke off into a sobs. With the worst of it over and the excitement at its end, my dwindling adrenaline left stone cold exhaustion in its wake.

"Christ. I'm so sorry I was gone, Leigh. I'm sorry," he whispered against my hair. He hugged me tight in his arms and refused to let go until my shaking ended. Afterward, we both walked to Sophia's room together. Even though the paramedics and I had both checked her, Ian looked her over himself.

It seemed like hours had passed before the cops were gone. The damage left from the firefight and failed drive-by made Ian reluctant to remain overnight.

"We're going to Gram's for the night. I'm not making you guys stay here. Pack up."

He didn't have to suggest the idea twice. It took about twenty minutes to pack up a bag and everything Sophia would need for a night away from home.

"Have you heard from Russ and Dani yet?"

Ian glanced down at his phone and shared the recent text message from Russ with me. "She's good, see? Russ is with her now and he says it's nothing major."

"She was so brave, Ian. You should have seen her." I wiped my eyes and got ahold of myself before I broke down, determined to be a strong wife Ian could be proud of. "I still don't know what happened outside, but there were growls. I thought maybe Trigger got loose and came to our rescue."

"I can explain, but it'd be better if you see it. Come on."

Ian picked up Sophia in her car seat and shouldered the diaper bag. He led the way to the forested walking path between the two houses while I led Petunia on a leash.

"Are you sure it's safe out here? Those snarls were so close."

"Trust me." Ian brushed a kiss against my temple then led me deeper onto the path. The last rays of sunlight cast shadows all around, but we weren't in complete darkness and the trees shielded us from the wind.

"Okay, lovebirds, you can come out now."

"Lovebirds?"

Leaves rustled to my left. As my gaze snapped from Ian's placid features, I caught sight of two wolves emerging from the brush. I staggered back a step and nearly lost my balance.

"It's okay, sweetie. They're with me."

"With you?" I questioned. My voice raised on the last word.

Both marvelous creatures moved forward to greet me with their proud heads raised. A rust-colored smear of dried blood stood out against the larger, charcoal and white-furred male wolf. The female had more blood around her blonde muzzle than he did, but no visible injuries. I never knew wolves could have green eyes.

"Ian, he's hurt." Petunia peeked out from behind my thigh at the two wolves. She didn't fear them as much as I expected.

"He'll be fine," Ian assured me. "Go on, guys. You don't have anything Leigh hasn't seen before."

The two wolves simultaneously canted their heads at Ian then glanced at me. The male had a skeptical look in his blue eyes.

"Seriously. Go ahead," Ian urged them.

The two animals underwent transformation, losing their fur and lupine shapes to rise onto their two hind legs. In the blink of an eye, they were a man and a woman barely any older than me. The girl wiped her mouth with the back of a wrist and grinned.

"You okay, Thomas?" Ian asked him.

"It hurt like a bitch, but I'll survive," Thomas replied. He glanced down at his side where a puckered, pink scar remained. My attention wavered between his muscles and the nude woman standing beside him.

She was classically beautiful by every definition of the word, with long, wavy golden hair. She had a fit, tanned body like a runner or tennis player.

"Thomas, there's a baby. Keep it clean," the blonde chastised with a slap against his arm.

Thomas chuckled and kissed her cheek. "Sure. Don't worry about being buck nekkid in front of her. Worry about my mouth."

"Meet my goddaughter, Ceres, and her mate, Thomas. They're going to help me with some problems in the area."

Ceres stepped forward instinctively to hug me then paused and dropped her arms at her sides. "Hi. Uh. I wish we met under better circumstances."

Don't look down, don't look down. My eyes involuntarily flicked down at Thomas' crotch. Were all shifters hung like horses? Hoping he hadn't noticed, I tore my gaze away to look at his face instead. He smirked at me, inspiring fears he could read my mind.

"You'll get used to it," Ceres assured me. "When Thomas first became a werewolf, it took us hours to coax him out of his clothes. He was so shy it was adorable. Anyway, how's your friend? Is she going to be okay? We watched EMS take her away, but we didn't want to risk anyone seeing us."

"She's definitely not coming home tomorrow," Ian said. "But her boyfriend says nothing critical was hit."

Ceres was right. As we talked, I found it easier to

ignore their nudity and to focus on the conversation. They walked with us down the forest path to Russ and Dani's house where we planned to borrow his truck for the night. He and Ian kept keys to each other's rides.

"We were on our way back from..." The girl's eyes drifted to Ian then back to me. "Anyway, we heard gunshots and knew they came from this direction."

"There was a third shooter about to come inside after your friend shot the other two. I distracted him so Ceres could catch him from the side," Thomas explained.

"Are you going to be okay?"

"Oh, yeah. I'm good. I'd rather be the one to get shot than Ceres anyway. It's a small price to pay."

"That last guy won't be using what's left of his hand for much." The corner of Ceres' mouth rose.

"I'll tell the police to keep an eye on local hospitals then," Ian said. "I can't thank you enough for coming to their rescue."

"No problem, man. We're going to hang around in this area and camp out. My cell is nearby, so we'll ring you if anything happens."

"Feel free to use my house if you need anything."

Ian fed a super condensed version of the story to his grandmother. By morning, it would probably be all over the news that a robbery had been foiled on a veteran's home in the country.

Ian hadn't fooled his grandmother, and he hadn't

fooled me either. The problem was trying to determine who he'd meant to convince with the story.

"Go have a soak in the tub, baby. I'll get Sophia her bottle and put her to bed."

Trusting him with my baby, I indulged in an hour-long soak until my skin became pruney, as if I could wash the terror of the day down the drain, too.

Ian wasn't in bed when I emerged from the bathroom, but Sophia was fast asleep with Petunia curled up beside her playpen. I found him on the porch, leaning against the rail with a pack of cigarettes in one hand and his phone in the other. I recognized the contemplative expression on his face.

"You smoke?"

Wearing a guilty expression on his face, he ceased swiping mid-text and glanced away. "I used to when I was a lot younger," he explained while tucking the device into his pocket. "While you were in the shower, I found Gram's stash. She tries to hide it, you know."

I nodded. "I smell it now and again mostly out here on the porch, so I sort of guessed she indulged."

Ian chuckled and set the pack on the porch railing. "Hell, she's over ninety years old. I figure she can do what she wants by now if it makes her happy, but she thinks it upsets me."

"Does it?"

"A little." He took a step closer to me and wrapped one arm around my shoulders. With one sweet kiss, my husband assuaged my worries and chased away the remnants of my fear. "Before you and Sophia came around, Gram and the team were all I had. I didn't retire from the Air Force because the career tired me, Leigh. I left because after Russel's wife died, I realized how fragile human life can be. I wanted to be around for her last years. She's... she *is* my mother. As close as I've ever had."

"I think Betty is too stubborn to leave you any time soon, Ian." I hugged him then leaned back to peer into his golden eyes. "Why are you out here alone?"

"Thinking."

"That much is apparent." I cupped his face in both of my hands and skimmed my thumb over the soft, silver-peppered scruff on his jaw. "If I'm going to be your wife and your mate, you need to trust me with the things troubling you. What's happening, Ian? I deserve to know as much and why someone tried to shoot me in my own home. Were you texting Russ? Is Dani okay?"

My husband dragged in a deep breath then guided me inside from the porch to the guest bedroom. Grateful to have him with me, I crawled beneath the sheets and tugged him in to join me. Sophia slept peacefully in the playpen beside us.

"Now spill it." Moving closer let me set my head on his shoulder, fanning my hair over his bicep and the pillow.

"Okay," he agreed. "Something is going wrong in this town, and I think the drug problem runs deeper than a few misguided kids dealing Xanax bars after school. It's worse than teens picking narcotics from the medicine cabinets of senior citizens. Someone put a hit out on me because I've been digging around in their business."

A hit. It was something straight out of one of his movies. The news should have terrified me, but instead, I felt a rare surge curiosity. "Are you going to clean up the town?"

"We're going to try. I made contact with a few people I work with. I don't trust the local police or the county boys."

"You don't think—"

"Maybe," he said. "Ceres bit someone hard enough to sever a blood vessel and some tendons. If they check into a hospital, I'll know about it. This problem in Quickdraw has gone on long enough."

"Is that why you decided to run for sheriff?"

"Partially. Everything I said about that before was true. If our own department is corrupt, then it needs to be cleaned out, top to bottom."

"I should be terrified right now, but..." A strange sense of levelheadedness pervaded my emotions, imploring me to remain calm. I'd first noticed it during the firefight between Daniela and the thugs. "I have nothing but absolute faith in you right now. Isn't that weird?"

"Of course you do."

"But why?" I raised my head from his shoulder.

"Along with turning into animals, we shifters have some, ahh... more passive abilities specific to our type of animal. As my bondmate you get to enjoy them whether I'm present or not for as long as I'm alive. You'll never suffer any kind of impairment — mental or physical — for long. And you'll be more rational than the average person."

"So," I began while twisting to roll onto his chest. It put our faces close, noses almost touching, eye to eye while I studied him in the dimmed bedroom lighting. Ian was an enigma, and nothing in the past prepared me for living life with a supernatural fantasy guy. "You're sexy, you turn into an eagle, filthy rich, good in bed, and you have some sort of magical healing aura?"

"Mmhmm. All eagles do. The Ojibwe believed we carried away sickness to the Creator. I wished I'd been there for Russ' wife, but we were both away so often together I never knew she was ill until she was beyond my help."

"Ian?"

"Hm?"

"Can Dani and I do the same thing now with the healing?"

"Yeah, you can, but not her. Why do you ask?"

"She was so brave," I repeated for what must have been the fifth time. "And she made me feel brave, too."

"Because she pulls it from Russ. He inspires bravery in others."

"One day, real soon, you're going to have to explain all of this to me because this is some need to know information."

Ian chuckled and opened his mouth to reply, only for the phone to buzz with an incoming message. Hiding nothing, he enabled the touch screen with a slide of his thumb and began reading the message.

We picked up your guy. You know where to meet us. We're on our way there.

~

IAN

*A*s I stepped down from the porch and approached Russ' truck, I shot a glance over my shoulder to the raven perched on the edge of the roof. Harrison would remain as lookout over the night, and he had strict instructions to warn Leigh if any suspicious activity occurred on his watch.

I left my wife with my pistol and the key to my grandmother's gun safe. After a five minute primer lesson on how to operate the handgun, Leigh's confidence skyrocketed. I wished we weren't in my grandmother's house and short on the time for hanky-panky. Seeing her with my gun turned me on.

Not once in all of my entire career had I ever used my privileges with the government for personal gain, but I was more than willing to use them to protect someone I loved. Leigh didn't know it, but all of our vehicles were tagged in law enforcement systems as special class federal vehicles. All six of us could speed to our heart's content with or without a siren, but we kept concealed equipment to use in emergencies. One button would blast sirens and flash lights. My foot remained anchored to the accelerator the entire way.

A black Mercedes awaited me at the safe house in the middle of the country, almost smack dab between Houston and San Antonio. Juni and Nadir occupied seats inside, one nibbling a stale donut and the other drinking coffee.

"Glad to have your help on this, Nadir. I know you just got home for your R&R." Nadir's Middle Eastern descent gave him the edge we needed during missions in Afghanistan. He'd spent the past two years in deep cover making sacrifices the rest of us couldn't imagine. Now he was home spending his first days lending me a hand.

Nadir scoffed and shook his head. "Don't think anything about it. We're family."

"Did he talk any yet?"

Nadir and Juni shook their heads.

"No," she said. "We waited for you. We didn't tell Russ we found him either, because we knew the moment we did, he'd rush out here from the hospital and we'd be lucky to have anything of him left for you to interrogate."

"Good thinking."

Juni worked Comms and Nadir was our Intel agent. Together, there wasn't much the two of them couldn't accomplish for the squad. I relied on them when legitimate methods of acquiring information were a bust or when I needed someone tracked down.

"How are we gonna do this one?" Juni asked. "The usual?"

I nodded and strode into the room to find my helpless target secured in a chair. He hyperventilated beneath the black hood, aware of the approaching footsteps.

"Who's there? Look, man, I need a doctor. Y'all gotta let me out of here. I didn't do nothin', you can't just hold me up in here like this."

Without concern for concealing my identity, I removed the black bag and stepped back until I came into focus for our captive. The man in the chair was slim, scrawny like most backwoods drug users. The partial halo of dark skin from repeated burns on the lower lip was the telltale sign of a crack addict, along with a half dozen other visible symptoms of drug dependency. Under these circumstances, pity wasn't part of my emotional repertoire.

"Ian MacArthur?"

I answered him with a sharp right hook to the face, juggling his head back and nearly knocking him unconscious. Usually, I was the calm and calculated one. The cool squad leader who never lost control. I had Russ' role today, and I played the part with ease.

This fucker could have killed my wife and child.

"Didn't expect to see me again, did you? Thought I was dead in there? Who sent you?"

"Fuck you," he spit out. "I know I got rights. Where's my lawyer?"

"I don't think you get how this works. There's no police involvement. No one, and I do mean no one, knows where the hell you are right now. You're a ghost no one will ever find, and judging from the looks of you, no one will ever miss. Now someone sent a truck load of you to my house to kill me, and I want to know who. *Now.*" Taking him by the shirt collar, I tightened the material until it cut into his throat. After giving him a ragdoll's treatment, his rebellion gave way to fear and he was thirsty for air again.

"I d-d-don't know much."

I cuffed him again, hard enough to knock the chair onto its back and for his head to strike the padded floor. We'd added that installation after Russ nearly cracked someone's skull open during an interrogation.

The guy had spit in Juni's face and the southern gentleman in Russ had exploded violently.

"Don't!" he shrieked, flinching away as I dropped to a knee beside his head with my fist raised.

"Ian!" Juni cried from the door. "What are you doing?"

"I'm fucking doing what needs to be done," I growled at her. My fist began its descent, but she ran forward and grabbed my arm at the elbow. Nadir hauled me back with one arm around my waist.

The scuffle ended with me in the control room after Juni shut the door in my face. I dropped into her chair at the computer console and watched them unfasten the bonds to release our prisoner. His limp, mangled hand had basic first aid to prevent bleeding out and little else, but I recognized Nadir's work. He and Sasha had worked closely during the final year of her active duty, making him our backup medic.

"Are you okay?" Juni asked gently. "I'm sorry, I really am." Our detainee had tears streaming down his face. I'd shaken him up good enough that he flinched back from her initially when she reached out. "I'm just going to have a look at your hand, okay? We want to get you some medical help, but I need you to cooperate first so I can help you."

"I'll get him something for the pain. He must feel awful right now," Nadir commented. He came out of the room and glanced at me after the door was shut. "Was all of it acting, or did you really lose it? That wasn't normal for you. You're always the cool-headed one."

So much for being calm and rational. "I really lost it for a second, but the end was acting," I admitted. We had a system here of good-cop, bad-cop, usually with Russ as the bad guy and one of the girls or Nadir as the good guy. The girls had the best luck thanks to their specific animal totems. Juni was our lucky rabbit and Sasha had the gift of timing. She always knew when to ask the right question.

"He's at ease with her already. Once she has him calmed down and comfortable, he'll spill whatever she wants." Nadir plucked a medical kit from the cabinet and dropped it on the table beside me.

"What are you giving him?" I watched him withdraw a small vial of clear liquid.

"Some morphine," Nadir replied. He withdrew a small amount of liquid, recapped the syringe, and returned to the room.

My operatives went through the usual song and dance. They got the guy comfortable and even got his name out of him. His name was Kevin Watson, and a quick look into our databases revealed he was the thirty-two-year-old, unemployed son of our town's bar owner with a history of possession charges.

"When do I get to leave?" I heard him ask. "I have

rights. I know I have rights. You guys can't keep me here like this, can you?"

"Soon, my friend. I promise it will all come to an end soon," Nadir assured him. "You're very fortunate Ian has the pull to keep you out of prison for your crimes. You participated in an attempted murder. Did you know an infant was in the room?"

"No, no. Montgomery never said anything about kids. He just said to go in hard if we saw MacArthur's vehicle parked in the drive. Told us the wife would be with his grandmother."

Bingo.

"Ask him about Chief Montgomery," I told Juni over the communication link. She wore a small earpiece while in the room with our suspect.

"It sounds like Montgomery really screwed you guys over," Juni said. She flashed the guy a sympathetic smile and pulled up a seat. "Does he normally do shit like that?"

"Hell yeah. Thinks he can get away with doing whatever he wants 'cause he's police chief."

Nadir whistled. "Sounds like a real asshole. Maybe there's a way we can help you and keep you safe. I guess if he knew you were talking to us, he'd have you locked up."

"He would. He knows people, man. I'll be in TDCJ and down at Ferguson Unit like my homie, DJ."

"DJ?" Nadir leaned forward a little on his seat.

"Dennis James. He got pinched by one of the honest cops. Uhh... What's his face... fucking Hunt caught him. Montgomery told us we're on our own if we get busted doing shit, and Dee got sloppy."

"Why didn't he try to make a deal? They gave him a pretty stiff sentence for the drugs he had on him, didn't they?"

"Yeah. That's 'cause Montgomery knows people. This place is fucked up, man. I knew it was over for him when he got sent to Ferguson. You can't hide once you're in there."

"I take it that means they have a few men on the inside."

Kevin nodded. "Yo, man, can I have another shot of whatever you gave me? The pain is starting to come back."

I chuckled. "Dose him up with something light and lemme make a couple calls. Our problem is bigger than I anticipated."

LEIGH

"*I*'d like to visit Daniela Reyes," I announced to the young woman at the nurses' station.

The cold, clinical environment of the county hospital surrounded me. Doors opened and closed, wafting the scent of chemical deodorizers.

Once I had directions to Dani's room, I made my way down the hall and knocked on the door.

"Come in!"

I stepped into a vacant room then shut the door behind me for privacy. The bathroom door was half ajar, but sour vomit assaulted my nose.

"Dani? You okay in there?" I hesitated outside the door, waiting to see if she wanted any help.

"Yeah. Just a sec, Leigh."

The toilet flushed, and then I heard her at the sink.

After a few swishes and gargles, Daniela's pasty face appeared in the doorway. "Sorry about that. Mind helping me back to the bed?"

Holding her gown shut in back with one hand, I helped the wobbling woman back into her bed. "You don't look so good. Hospital food not agreeing with you?" I expected to see Russ asleep in a chair. Rumpled hospital blankets were strewn over the back of it, indicating he'd been there. Tentative about making myself at home, I sat on the edge of the seat.

"The food is godawful. Russ went to get me McDonald's while the breakfast menu is available." Dani did a double take and looked around the room in confusion. "Where's Sophia?"

"With her great-grandmother. Betty assured me she can still change a diaper and swaddle an infant. Plus, she has Ian's goddaughter helping."

"Good, I'm glad everyone is safe. I heard an animal growling outside during the shootout, so I just assumed another you-know-who was involved."

I crept to the door and peeked into the hall. Without a nurse in sight, I took a minute to catch her up on the news. I told her about the wolves outside and the young man who knocked on our door that morning. His name was Harrison and he had kept watch over the house all night for Ian.

"Ohhh. Russ mentioned wolves coming to visit, but didn't say much." Dani's distracted demeanor was at odds with her usual bubbly personality, setting off my maternal instincts. She looked like she needed a hug, so I leaned in and gave her one, careful of her bandaged shoulder.

"I'm so sorry you were hurt, hon."

"You aren't the one who hurt me, Leigh. I just feel awful right now."

"Is everything okay? Should I call the doctor in? Would you like me to go and let you rest some more?"

"No. No doctor. It's... I'm pregnant. The hospital labs confirmed it for me after I arrived," Dani admitted. She picked at the edge of her hospital gown sleeve. "Russ doesn't know yet. I don't really know *how* to tell him."

The news caught me by surprise and my gut instinct to congratulate her hung on the tip of my tongue. "I'm going to go out on a limb and guess you guys weren't trying."

Dani shook her head. "I had an IUD in, but you know how the doctors tell you there's always a tiny, insignificant chance they can fall out or become ineffective? Mine's gone. I never even noticed."

"Are you gonna tell him soon?"

"I think so. I don't — do you think he'll be happy?"

"Dani, he'll be ecstatic. The question is, are *you* happy? Are we celebrating this baby? Do we get to go hog-wild at the mall buying booties and blankies when you get out of here?"

A fragile smile surfaced on Dani's face. I relaxed immediately. "I think so. I lost a baby once, you know. When I was married to my ex-husband, the one I killed two years ago. The doctors gave me the whole song and dance about it being a natural occurrence sometimes. Said nothing could have prevented it." She shook her head. "Michael blamed me for losing his son."

My belly knotted in worry again. "Is this baby going to be okay?" I gestured to her bandaged shoulder.

"Thanks to you, I didn't lose as much blood as I could have. He or she seems fine." She nibbled her lower lip and glanced down at her tummy. "They're going to send an ultrasound tech in around noon to check. I have until then to tell Russ."

"He'll be thrilled, Dani, I just know it."

Maybe his ears were burning, because Russell chose that moment to push through the door. Two large takeout bags and a cup holder with coffee and orange juice filled his big hands.

"You didn't answer your phone, and I wasn't sure what you wanted... so I grabbed two of everything," he called out, setting the food and drinks on the table. "Oh, hey, Leigh."

"Morning, Russ. I came to check on Dani and we got to chatting."

"Sorry I took so long, darlin'. I ran home to feed

Trigger and Daisy, too." He looked like hell with dark circles under his eyes. He fidgeted more than usual.

Dani fetched a hash brown out of the bag. "Go ahead and have some, Leigh. I can't eat all of this and neither can Russ."

"Sorry, I wasn't really thinking when I placed the order." Russ' boyish grin wiped the nervousness from his face.

Poor guy. He must be so worried about Dani.

Russ lowered Dani's hospital rail out of his way and sat beside her on the bed while she dug into her biscuit sandwich. I helped myself to the spare. We all ate together and made idle chat until Russ began talking all in a rush.

"Dani, I love you. I was planning to wait until Christmas to lay this on you, but there's no time like the present, right?" He rubbed his hand up and down her thigh over the blanket. She gave him an odd look.

"Russ, what are you talking about? No time to do what? To give me breakfast?"

The bearshifter shook his head and fetched a black box from his windbreaker pocket. My eyes — and Dani's too — darted to his open palm immediately. All of my concentration became devoted to not inhaling a piece of egg.

"You're more than my mate, darlin'. You're my soul and the air I breathe. Living with you isn't enough anymore for me. I want you to be my wife. Marry me."

He opened the box to reveal a sparkling ruby surrounded by diamond-encrusted leaves. The gold setting glimmered in the diffuse hospital room light.

I had been granted the privilege of witnessing a beautiful moment. Tears burned my eyes and I held my breath, knowing Dani's answer before it came from her lips.

"Russ…" Tears streamed down her face. "Yes! Oh, my god, yes! But there's something you need to know first."

"What is it, darlin'? You can tell me anything."

"Remember how I haven't been feeling well lately? The ER doctor ordered some tests before you got here last night. I'm pregnant."

"I'm going to be a father?" The joy on Russ' face was almost painful to see. Sophia's father hadn't looked so happy when I told him I was pregnant.

I dreamed of a day when I could relay the same news to Ian. Sophia was my world, but fantasies raced through my thoughts of giving my husband a child with his shifter heritage — a little sister or brother to grow up alongside Sophia. As Russ doted over his wife-to-be, I eased from my seat and crept to the door. I pulled it shut behind me to grant them privacy.

Once I fished my phone out, I asked Ian via text if it was safe to call. My phone rang less than a minute later when I reached the hospital elevator.

"What's up, sweetie?" The sound of his tired voice thrilled me.

"I'm so glad you're okay. You've been quiet since you drove off last night, and I worried about you," I babbled out.

"I'm fine. We'll be on our way back to Quickdraw soon. How's Dani?"

"Engaged and pregnant," I chirped, unable to hold the news to myself.

"Hot damn. Tell 'em I said congrats."

"We'll have to do it later. I snuck on out before Russ had the chance to begin bawling over her."

Ian's rich laughter warmed my heart. I leaned against the side of the elevator and closed my eyes. "I miss you."

"I miss you too, baby. Thomas and Ceres are behaving, right?"

"Thomas didn't show up this morning, but Ceres and Harrison came in to eat breakfast when I left Betty's house. She said he found a peculiar smell by the river bottoms and wanted to loop back one more time."

"Sounds like Thomas. They're good kids—"

"Ian, they're older than I am. Stop calling them kids."

"Habit," he admitted. His sheepish laugh painted a picture in my mind of his broad smile and glinting eyes.

I stepped out of the elevator to the ground floor and moved for the parking lot. "Tell me the truth, Ian. I know you can't go into details, but I need to know if you're going into something dangerous."

First he was silent, then I heard him inhale a deep breath. "It'll be dangerous, but I promise, I'll be home to you."

"That's all I need to know. Let me know when it's over."

"I will. Do one favor for me. Tell Russ to check his cellphone. I'm calling the squad together."

~

IAN

"Why the fuck was I excluded?" Russ demanded.

"Because Dani needed you, and we knew you'd fly off the handle," I said.

Russ appeared less than impressed with my response, but as the squad leader, I called the shots and chose team members.

"Fine," he grumbled. "I just wish you'd trusted me enough to tell me what was going on."

"Ian trusts you, Russ. You know that, just as much as we all know how much you love Dani. Our informant would be a smear on the concrete floor if you were there during the interrogation." Sasha set her hand on Russ' shoulder. "Be reasonable."

"I said fine." The cross expression faded from his face. "I am fine. Sorry. I just get so angry where Dani is concerned. Can't help it, guys."

Once his cooler head prevailed, we returned to our debriefing.

"Our informant tells us there are a handful of small-time dealers, but the guys we really want are woven into the Quickdraw PD and our county sheriff's department. There's a couple in the higher echelon." I slid my finger over the touch display and opened an image. "Chief Montgomery ordered the hit. My snooping around in his town and asking questions scared him. They know if I run for sheriff in the next election, they don't have a chance in hell of bribing me to shut up."

"Yeah, because you're already making legitimate money hand over fist," Juni chirped. "You don't need their payoffs."

"Ian's incorruptible," Nadir added. "They have good reason to be scared."

"Do we have authorization?" Sasha asked. "We need to do this by the book if we're going to go in."

"We have everything we need. Unless your hands —" I gave a pause to look at Sasha "—or your paws are forced, we're not to engage in combat. We don't want a meth lab of dead junkies with claw marks in them. This isn't Baghdad and we're not at war."

"Look, I can't be held responsible for that," Sasha said. "I'm sorry I almost broke cover that day, but I don't regret killing them all."

"Nice kitty," Nadir murmured.

Sasha hissed at him.

"If you're in a bind, by all means, let your claws out. I want to go in hard, get the evidence we need, and get out. Subdue if possible before taking any lives."

"If the sheriff is in on all this, who are you planning on handing the evidence over to?" Taylor tucked a knife inside his boot.

"Texas Rangers. I called my friend, Charles, to give us a hand. He's on his way out from Dallas," I explained.

Juni's eyes grew round. "You have friends in the Rangers, too?"

"Ian has friends everywhere. You should know that by now, darlin'." Russ clapped Juni on the shoulder.

"Officially, it's their case, but we're gonna make it all easy for them and have this wrapped up nice and tight by the time they arrive." I rose from my seat and passed out earpieces. "Juni spent a lot of time making these to fit our unique shapes. They're for us to use in our animal forms."

Sasha stared at the circular device I handed her. "Ian, this is a cat collar."

"It's extendable, Sasha. It'll adjust whenever you shift." Juni opened her laptop and logged into her tracking program. "With this, I'll be able to follow all of you. We tagged the wolves and their ravens already. If you swap to your human form to communicate, I'll be here at Ian's place to direct you."

"Sounds good," Russ said. He turned his collar around in his hands a few times then tried to fasten it around his neck.

"That's for your wrist, Russ," Juni said.

"Oh."

"Taylor, since you, Ian, and Russ are the only animals native to this area, I'm counting on you to get as close as you can without provoking them to put a bullet in your ass," Nadir said. "I'm staying behind with Juni to operate the video systems."

"Sweet. I can do that. You just want some good surveillance feed as evidence, right?" Taylor asked.

"Right. We need clear visuals on faces and activities," Juni replied.

Once preparations were made, our team split. Juni and Nadir remained behind at my place to run the control center, but I had the most difficult job of them all: I refused to allow anyone to confront Montgomery before me.

~

"About time you got here," Kevin complained. His voice crackled through the wire we'd taped to his chest. I listened from my hiding spot outside of a leaning shack in the woods.

Confronting Sheriff Montgomery wasn't enough. We needed him to freely confess what he'd done. My contacts with the Texas Rangers had approved the ruse, lending legitimacy to evidence I planned on collecting.

"Where the hell have you been, Kevin?"

"Taking care of my damn hand, man. You didn't say MacArthur had fuckin' attack dogs. You gave us bad info, Sheriff."

"You assured me you and your boys could handle MacArthur," Sheriff Montgomery spat. "If you can kill him, you could have shot a couple mutts."

"Well, he wasn't there. Just pay up and I'll go."

"I'm not paying you for an unfinished job. You were sent to kill MacArthur and his junkie slut. That's what I hired you for. Last I checked they were alive and your boys were arrested. Such a shame they tried to escape and were shot."

"We told you we weren't gonna kill Leigh! You promised she wouldn't be there. I only went because you swore he'd be alone. I can't go back there again! He'll be expecting it. I can't even hold a gun right now. Look at my hand."

I smirked. Ceres didn't play around when it came to taking someone down. He was lucky to have escaped with his throat intact. Hell, he'd be lucky to make any sort of deal at all to keep from going away to prison for life.

"Then I guess you're no use to me anymore, Kev."

"Hey, man... what the fuck? Put the gun down!"

As much as Kevin deserved to get shot, this wasn't the way to do things. I needed him on a witness stand. Abandoning my post outside, I circled round to the front and kicked the door in.

I had a split second to make my decision. The gun swung around toward me, but my sharp reflexes gave me ample time to twist out of the bullet's path. It struck the wall behind me instead, shattering the glass in a picture frame. I usually saved the inhuman reflexes for the battlefield when there weren't any witnesses left to tell tales. For Montgomery, I made an exception. I was on him in a second, smashing my knuckles into his chin. He stumbled back and lost control of his gun when I twisted his arm and dislocated his shoulder to disarm him. Kevin, the junkie we'd used as our bait, high-tailed it out the door without a backward glance.

Unwilling to go without a fight, the sheriff swung his heavy fist around and clipped me in the temple. I blocked another punch and flipped him to the floor.

The chunky, out of shape police chief didn't have a chance against me, but I lacked mercy.

"You sent men to kill my wife." My fist pounded into his face, cracking cartilage in his nose. My eagle craved vengeance *and* his blood, demanding his death for daring to put my mate in danger.

"Ian," Juni spoke up through the communication channel.

Montgomery groaned, his attempt to speak coming out as a hoarse croak.

"You're going to pay for what you've done here, Montgomery. All this time, you knew about the bull-shit happening here." I punched him again, bruising my knuckles. He grunted and spit blood to the side.

"Ian, stop!" Juni cried. "You'll kill him if you keep up like this."

"Maybe I want to kill him," I growled out.

"You don't," she disagreed, adopting the placid tone reserved for our detainees.

"She's right, Ian," Nadir said. "Listen to us. You do not want this man's blood on your hands. You're better than that."

Montgomery's head lolled back. Blood trickled from his nose and split lip, and all I wanted was to finish what I began.

"Fine," I hissed between my teeth. I waited for the anger to recede, breathing in deep and measured breaths. Even my eagle had been ready to surrender to our shared anger, enraged by the man's decision to place Leigh and Sophia in danger. "Get to talking, Montgomery. Tell me everything."

"Ian. Ian, you don't understand. There are things going on in this town that you can't comprehend. Things you won't want to be involved in. You'll wish he killed you and Leigh both if you go through with this."

"Right now, my squad is leading a raid against three different meth labs and crack houses set up in the boonies. We're taking your supply line down."

"You'll never find the supply line. Those are only decoys. They don't mean anything."

"Then tell me where to find the real source. Tell me now and it'll look good on you later when the DA presses charges against you. Maybe they'll cut you a deal."

Montgomery's bitter chuckle unnerved me and shattered my righteous indignation. "You can't stop what's happening here. No one can."

"You won't be able to get any information from him, Ian. That guy's out of it. Give it up," Nadir said.

"Yeah, you're right," I replied. I stood and left Montgomery on the floor to look out the window. There wasn't any sign of Kevin. "Our witness is gone."

"I saw it," Juni reassured me. "Thomas has him cornered outside." The wolf growled low to confirm. "Your help is on the way, Ian, not that you need them."

"Sit your ass on the floor until the Rangers get in here to arrest you," I barked at him.

I patted Montgomery down and found a second firearm concealed in his boot. About five minutes later, tires screeched on the blacktop to herald my backup's timely arrival. Somehow, I hadn't given in to my bestial nature. Death was more than he deserved for everything he'd done.

Montgomery's wet cough held too much amusement for my taste. Crossing to the window, I glanced outside at the two trucks with their flashing lights. Once I verified my friend was one of the responding officers, I pulled open the door and stepped outside.

Shamed and stripped of his authority, Montgomery surrendered to his own cowardice in the early hours of the morning a week later. Officers found him hanging by a bed sheet in a cell. He'd taken his secrets with him.

EPILOGUE

FOUR MONTHS LATER

IAN

"Leigh? Baby? I'm back."

Three weeks away from my wife and daughter felt like a lifetime. I loved my job and hiring out my services to the government, but for the first time in my entire career, I couldn't wait to be home.

Following the dramatic end of Chief Montgomery's reign over Quickdraw, the drug trade calmed down and the remaining police officers quietly resumed cleaning up my hometown. Everyone knew about my upcoming campaign for County Sheriff, and thanks to the part I played in bringing the crooked chief to justice, my election was guaranteed.

Shortly after Leigh, Sophia, and I spent our first

Christmas together, I resumed taking government contracts. Russ and I planned to build a comfortable savings account to allow us to remain home for the unforeseeable future. He wanted to spend the next year with Dani and their child. I wanted to be there for Leigh to provide the support she needed.

This is it. The last job until Leigh's out of school. Nothing to stand between her and me now. And even then maybe I am done for good. Maybe it's time to retire and pass the torch to Nadir. Maybe it's time to become a real family man and run things from behind the scenes.

It was time to end my career. For Leigh and Sophia, I'd give up anything.

I stepped through the door, eager to pull my two favorite girls into my arms. Once I found them. Leigh's scent led me to the backyard and I leaned against the door, watching. She had a large blanket spread out over the grass and Sophia playing beside her. Petunia napped in the sun nearby along with the single puppy we'd kept. Wedding magazines piled up within her reach, another sight that brought a smile to my face. Russ and I had been in full agreement with the girls' plan for a double wedding.

I wanted Leigh to have the fairy tale ceremony she deserved.

"Hey, beautiful," I called out loud enough to catch her attention.

"Ian!" Leigh jumped to her feet and met me

halfway across the yard. Her kisses welcomed me home; the joy surpassed only by the toothless grin Sophia gave me from the blanket.

"I didn't expect you back so early."

"Well, we managed to wrap everything up sooner than expected. A couple of the guys hung around to play at being tourists, but Russ and I couldn't wait," I indulged her in another kiss, "to return where we belong." Now that Dani was in her approaching her third trimester, Russ didn't plan to take another job for a while.

"Da da da da." Sophia clapped and held her arms up toward me when we approached. I scooped her up and kissed her cheek.

"Yup, I'm home, princess." Tiny hands touched my face and unshaven jaw. Patting my cheeks, my soon-to-be adopted daughter gazed deep into my eyes.

"Da daaaaa."

"I hope you love me as much when I'm chasing boys off our porch with a shotgun sixteen years from now."

"Ian." Leigh swatted me.

"I'm joking." With both of us around to teach her good from bad, hopefully, I'd never need to do it.

"I was about to take her inside for naptime."

"I'll carry her up," I volunteered. Both dogs roused and followed on my heels, dancing behind me every step of the way.

Sophia settled in for her afternoon nap without fuss, as if she'd been waiting for me to tuck her in. Leigh met me at the bottom of the stairs, shaking her head.

"She always falls asleep so quickly when you do it," she complained.

"I have a way with women."

"Come back outside with me, the day is beautiful."

Leigh pulled me by the hand to the patio. I chuckled at the college textbooks piled on the table. "How's the schoolwork going?"

"Great, actually. Dani proofread my essay, and I have a project I have to give for some of the senior citizens at the assisted living center near school."

"Yeah? What's it on?" With encouragement from Sasha, Dani, and even me, Leigh had returned to school. I couldn't be prouder. She'd graduate with her degree in another semester.

"The healing properties of music therapy and its effect on individuals with Alzheimer's disease." She rattled out a mouthful of words that made me grin. Leigh had an amazing singing voice to begin with, but she was thrilled to discover her area of study benefitted from our bonding. She wanted to use the powers transferred through our link to help others as a music therapist.

I whistled. "Sounds like good stuff."

Leigh's cheeks colored. "It is, I think. Will you listen and be my guinea pig before I go perform?"

"Of course. You know how much I love to hear your voice."

She blushed again, a trait I never tired of. "There's something else, actually."

"Yeah? What is it, hon?"

"While you were gone, I got myself a new doctor and had a visit."

"Are you sick?" A concerned wrinkle creased my brow. I glanced my wife over as if any illness would be visible in her appearance, still haunted by the memory of Katie Hawkins sunken cheeks and thinning hair. She'd tried to endure chemotherapy without Russ, afraid informing her husband of her illness would recall him from active duty to be at her side. Maybe it was too early to make the determination that I couldn't live without Leigh at my side, but I could easily and honestly say I didn't *want* to be without her.

"No, silly." Leigh only laughed before giving me a reassuring pat to one thigh. "I visited the lady doctor. I, um... had something put in." She showed me the tiny scar on her arm and guided my fingers to touch the slim, hard presence beneath her skin. "I didn't know how you felt about kids, but I know Sophia is all I need right now."

"Leigh—"

She held up a hand to show she wasn't finished.

"Right now, Ian. But one day after I'm out of school, if you'd like me to get it removed, I'd like that too," she whispered.

"A little sibling for Sophia."

Leigh nodded. "Yes. I want a baby with you, enough that I kept thinking about it." Heat suffused to her face, bringing a rush of pink color. "But even more, I want to feel you without anything between us. No more condoms."

Certain traits of a shifter's personality were ruled by our animal aspects, driving us to mate frequently to preserve our species. The arrival of spring brought mating season for eagles, a sensitive time for me. I was completely erect in the time it took to rise from my seat. Maybe she didn't want the child now, but the only thing concerning my eagle was her confession of desire. She'd said it. She wanted my baby.

"I need to be inside you right now." I fumbled with my belt, but then Leigh took over. She had my pants lowered and my cock out within seconds. I'd never been so hard in all of my life.

"Fuck," I swore out loud when she took me into her mouth. Her lips formed a perfect ring around my dick, teasing only the tip with her tongue. It was the worst and best kind of torture. I wanted to fuck her so deep and so hard she saw stars.

"Leigh, baby, how long? Do I need backup?"

Her mouth came off me with a wet pop. "No. It's

been in long enough." Leigh's hand slid over my ass and squeezed. One forward movement slid my cock into her mouth again. I watched it disappear inch by inch until her nose nestled against the base of my dick and my balls touched her chin. My head tilted back in ecstasy.

I was already close to the edge before she began bobbing back and forth. Skilled fingers teased my balls, and then she pulled back. Her lips pressed against my hip while she left my dick exposed to the air.

"I love what you're doing to me, baby, but I need to be inside of you. Right now."

We didn't waste time; Leigh's clothes fell away between our united efforts. One swift yank pulled her against me, her back to my chest and her ass cradling my dick. She wriggled against me, sliding up and down until I couldn't take it anymore and bent her forward.

Without a condom to separate us, I snapped my hips forward and drove into her. The exquisite sensation of her pussy surrounded me all at once, and required me to linger in place, buried balls deep in her body. I couldn't move, overcome by how amazing she felt. Our fit was puzzle piece perfection, like two halves of the same whole merging together once more. When she adapted to my size, I set a fast rhythm like our usual lovemaking. I needed a hot and fast fucking, a primal mating to assert my claim of her. She could do whatever she wanted to me later, but right now, her pussy belonged to me.

"*Mine,*" I hissed out between my teeth, while Leigh moaned and clutched onto the edge of the patio table. I didn't care that we were outside, her bared ass exposed, her gorgeous tits jiggling for anyone to see. I throbbed inside her and experienced every tremble of her walls. "Tell me you're mine."

"Yours, baby. I'm yours. I'll always be yours," she panted out.

If I could have called in victory like an eagle, I would have. Instead, I groaned my pleasure against the shell of her ear.

"Touch me, Ian," she pleaded. "I want your hands on my breasts."

I teased her full tits, pulling and rolling each pink tip between my fingertips, visualizing them in my hands. Each one was a perfect palmful. Leigh moaned and rocked back against me, her hands clutching the patio table edge for support. Keeping one hand on her breasts, squeezing and kneading, I slid the other down her side to her hip. The lush curve received a light smack, and then I gripped her thigh and plunged within her body with renewed vigor.

Flesh slapped against flesh as we both gave in to our carnal desires. My wife's fast, breathy pants climbed higher and higher in pitch. Leigh's pussy tightened around my cock, a vice-like grip that pushed me over the edge.

"Sweet God, Leigh, I love you so much."

I gave her the words in my heart as I tightened in orgasm behind her, releasing burst after burst of my seed inside her body's tight embrace. Leigh reached back with one arm and hooked it around my neck. We held each other close and rode out the aftershocks together, until she was limp and pliant in my hold.

I carried her off the wooden deck into the sweet smelling clover. After I sank to my knees and lowered Leigh to lie beside me, I held her close and secure in my arms. We didn't move from where we lay in the grass, naked as the day we were born, our legs entwined and bodies close. We exchanged lazy, drugging kisses that made me linger on the border of sleep, and then I made love to her again face to face with one of her legs over my hip. Taking it slow gave me the chance to lavish her breasts with tender affection. I trapped one nipple between my teeth, stimulating the tender peak until her pussy clenched around my dick and she shuddered in orgasm.

"I'm so glad you're home again," she whispered against my cheek when both of our breaths had slowed.

"Me too, sweetheart." I didn't dare to part from her, leaving my half-hard dick surrounded by her warmth.

"It feels so good to make love to you without a condom." So good I couldn't bear to leave.

"Mmhmm," she agreed. "Can't wait to see you in your uniform for the wedding." She ran her fingers down my chest.

Having Leigh in my arms, her body nestled in close, was everything I wanted.

"Tell me again, what you said before."

"I love you," I whispered, dropping a kiss on her lips.

"I love you, too, Ian. With all my heart."

Somehow, fate had brought two lost souls together. Sophia and Leigh completed me, the family I'd needed and looked for all my life. They were worth fighting for, and for them, I'd finish what the team and I began in November. The town may have become quieter in the wake of Chief Montgomery's suicide, but I wouldn't rest until the remaining dealers were off the streets.

I couldn't rest until our hometown was the place Sophia and our future children deserved.

OTHER BOOKS BY VIVIENNE

Fairy Tale Retellings

For the reader who likes their romance milder

Beauty and the Beast

Red and the Wolf

Goldilocks and the Bear

Belle and the Pirate

Dragons

For the reader who likes their romance smutty

Loved by the Dragon

Smitten: Dawn of the Dragons #2

Crush on a Dragon: Dawn of the Dragons #3

God of Mischief: Dawn of the Dragons #4

Military Shifters

Hot and Wild military alphas

The Right to Bear Arms (Book #1)

Let Us Prey (Book #2)

The Purr-fect Soldier (Book #3)

Old Dog New Tricks (Book #4)

Impractical Magic

Milder romance for the reader who loves action

Impractical Magic

Better Than Hex (Impractical Magic #2)

Blood Heiress

It's all about the plot and a slow burn relationship

<u>Blood Kissed</u>

Werewolves of San Antonio

<u>Training the Alpha</u>

Mythological Creatures

Making Waves

OTHER BOOKS BY PAYNE & TAYLOR

Epic Fantasy by Dominique Kristine

Shadows for a Princess

A princess who would rather die than wed. A warrior priest who would rather kill than see her harmed. A kingdom of shadows and treachery that threatens them both...

At the age of twenty-eight, Princess Ysolde Westbrook is a spinster duchess, the adopted daughter of Hindera's eccentric monarch. Commoners love their benevolent leader, but the kingdom's gentry take offense to the outsider among them. Amid noble plots and demands for her to marry a local aristocrat, an assassination attempt places her life in peril--if she will not have one of them for a husband, they would sooner see her dead.

Finding allies in strangers with powerful gifts and even darker secrets, Ysolde must learn what it means to lead and find her own inner strengths. Whether or not she survives the tangled web of treason will determine the fate of her duchy, the royal family, and the kingdom she loves.

Blend the intrigue of Game of Thrones with a touch of Outlander's romance for an adventurous fantasy in a whole new realm of magic. Fans of Diana Gabaldon and George R.R. Martin will love the richly descriptive world of Terraina.

SAVED BY THE DRAGON

Thunder cracked overhead, a grim herald of what was to come. Barely a minute later, the sky seemed to split open and unleash a torrent of freezing cold rain. And Chloe Ellis was caught without her umbrella, clutching a rocky wall nearly a hundred feet off the ground.

Shit!

She hadn't anticipated the weatherman's predicted 20% chance of rain would come with a furious thunderstorm. Within an hour of her climb, dark clouds had swept over the topaz blue skies and eclipsed the sun. Lightning flashed in the distance.

"Well damn, what do I do now?" She wedged her body into the crack leading toward the high summit, hoping to escape the brunt of the wind and rain.

Of the three options available to her, none held any

appeal. She could stay hanging where she was and hope the rain passed soon, attempt to make her way down, or keep pressing for the cliffs.

Wiping water from her face, she gazed around for an alternative. The fissure in the rock face widened several feet above her, so she made her way up and breathed a quiet prayer of thanks for the small ledge at the top. It was a place to rest safely and wait out the storm.

The narrow shelf extended farther than she'd thought at first glance. Chloe wriggled back into the crawlspace to get out of the rain. Loose grit shifted beneath her hands, skittered down a dark passage. She fetched a flashlight from her backpack and eased down the crumbling slope. Water ran in narrow rivulets from the mountain shelf behind her, plastering her hair to the back of her neck.

Should have brought Freddy with me, she thought. *Now, I'm here alone, and hiding from the rain.*

Freddy, her on-again off-again boyfriend, had practically begged to come along on this trip. He wanted to work things out; promised he'd be a changed man. They could camp and make love under the stars. Of course, he was only the most recent train wreck in a chain of failed romances.

Before Freddy, she had dated Malcolm; the hottie at the law firm where she practiced her paralegal work. Dating him had been a dream. He had a sweet personality, a stable income as a lawyer, and he seemed to love her dearly.... Until she returned a day ahead of schedule from a visit to care for her ailing father.

Chloe had walked into their shared home to discover Malcolm urging his weekend lay to hide in the closet.

Four years. She swept it all down the drain that day and refused to hear out his ridiculous excuses about becoming too drunk to say no. How he'd come out to drink with pals, who later wouldn't excuse his behavior and ratted him out because they'd warned him not to do it. Three of them broke the bro code in an effort to step in for their friend.

So she went against her better judgment and began to date Freddy; Malcolm's physical trainer, and a man with a body like an Olympian. The sex was great, and the way he treated her was even better.

Or so it had seemed.

Their first fight came four months into the relationship when his jealous persona arose. He didn't want her to have male friends because it wasn't appropriate, and no man merely wanted to be her friend. They'd want to fuck her too. They had another fight in the days prior to her little decision to go away for a weekend alone.

What made me think I could do this alone without him? It was foolish, dumb, and dangerous, Chloe thought. Freddy knew what he was doing on the mountain peaks. They'd bonded over a mutual lust for the outdoors during the initial stages of their dating. It wouldn't have been the first time they went away for a weekend in the wilderness.

The pebbles beneath her feet shifted. She slid forward and lost her balance, and in the process of attempting to regain her footing, landed heavily on her butt and slid down the cave's treacherous slope like a reluctant toddler at the playground. She screamed all the while and scraped her nails uselessly against the rocky wall at either side. Eventually, she reached the end and became airborne.

All sense of time fell away as Chloe tumbled through the air with the debris from the shaft, arms and legs flailing uselessly at the air like a baby bird falling from its nest the first time. Merciless and unyielding rock caught her, although she landed on her ankle and crumpled soon after. White-hot pain exploded through her entire leg; worse than anything she'd ever experienced before.

"Fuck!" she swore, loudly, after all who would hear. Her flashlight tumbled from her hands and rolled across the cavern floor. The wobbling light danced over the rough-hewn walls in a dizzying display until the small device rolled to a stop. She'd have to crawl to reach it and risk scraping her knees and hands to high hell in the process.

Nearly thirty minutes had passed before she was

able to stop crying. Instead of feeling strong and adventurous, she felt weak and miserable. Her wet clothes and the damp environment worsened her ordeal. Of course, Chloe had also learned a very valuable lesson about adventuring without a partner.

After a while she climbed up from the ground and gingerly tried to apply weight to her left ankle. A merciless twinge, striking her joint with the ferocity of a hammer blow, forced her to immediately draw her foot off the ground again. The nearby stalagmite became her leaning post while she waited for the nausea to settle.

"Okay. Chloe, think," she told herself, while salty tears leaked down her cheeks. Her voice echoed across the cavern. "This is a popular climb. I just need to... to wait for the rain to stop and listen. Call for help."

It wasn't in her plans to die alone and in the dark recesses of some unknown cave. Unfortunately, cell phone signals wouldn't reach the outside world. She confirmed it at a glance.

Once she eased down to the cave floor, Chloe tried to pull herself together. A search through her pack produced a basic first aid kit, emergency blanket, a few energy bars, and some dehydrated meals. Being injured didn't change the fact that her activities had provoked a ravenous hunger that couldn't be sated by a tiny little rectangle of granola and dried cranberries that she had brought with her.

She rifled through the first aid kit and removed the small bottle of ibuprofen. She popped two into her mouth and swallowed them dry. The Band-Aids and antibiotic cream were useless, so she shoved the box back into her bag and leaned against the cavern wall to wallow in her misery. This vacation sucked. Freddy was probably getting his dick sucked by some ditzy bitch in a pink sports bra and booty shorts while she suffered in the dark.

"Have you become lost?"

The voice promptly shook her from a daydreaming state.

Or maybe I'm hallucinating...

The shirtless man who stepped into her field of vision belonged in a gym commercial with his rippling muscles and washboard abs. His wavy blonde hair touched his broad shoulders and curled at the tips, and a reddish scruff covered his jawline. Although her tastes usually ran to black hair and blue eyes like tall, dark, and handsome Freddy, something about the fair-haired stranger lured her like a siren's call.

She would definitely make an exception for the bearded Viking in the cave.

"Are you among the hearing impaired?"

"What?" Delusions weren't supposed to speak, were they? The sudden realization that help had arrived filled her with relief. Chloe pushed to her feet and promptly cried out. Her forward stumble knocked her straight into the stranger's strong arms.

"You are injured."

"My ankle," she sobbed. She hadn't realized how cold she was until held in his embrace. The man radiated heat like the sun on a cloudless summer day. Given the dire need to become warm, she had no reservations about wriggling in against his chest. The thought did occur to her that she should ask why a random, sexy stranger was in a dark cave system - and shirtless - until she saw the incredibly heavy backpack at his feet.

Maybe he was an axe murderer hiding out from the police, and planned to kill and eat her over his own camp fire. Hell if she knew, but at least she'd get warm before he did it.

ABOUT THE AUTHOR

Vivienne Savage is the pen name of two best friends who write everything together. One works as a nurse in a rural healthcare home in Texas and the other is a U.S. Navy veteran. Both are mothers to two darling boys and two amazing girls.

All of their work varies in steam level, so pop by the VS website for details on which series is right for you!

For more information

www.viviennesavage.com

vivi@viviennesavage.com